1

STARS
SHINE
IN
KEFALOS

By

Wendy

Howard

STARS SHINE IN KEFALOS

Woodrow Publishing

www.woodrowpublishing.com/

ISBN: 9798871897546

A note from the Author

To those of you, who have bought the books which make up the Stars Trilogy, I thank you. And for those of you who gave me such positive feedback, may I also say thank you. I did not intend to write a fourth book, but so many of you asked me to continue with the story that I had to, so here it is.

The first chapter is a summary, in a way, of Jenny, the lady who started the dynasty by moving to Kefalos. It explains how some of the characters also came to live there on the island.

If you have read all three books, then I hope this will refresh your memory of how the family has evolved over the years, and the episodes in their lives which have led them to call Kefalos their home.

I hope you will enjoy reading this book just as much as I enjoyed writing it.

Kind regards

Wendy

Acknowledgments'

I would like to thanks those friends who have helped me with the content of the story.

Special thanks to Dave for all his help

Credit to THOMAS organisation who provided information about rehabilitation programmes, and to the Phoenix hub who work with vulnerable and homeless people.

Thank You

Wendy

Contents

CHAPTER 1
THE GARDEN OF HER DREAMS

As Jenny sat on the balcony in her rocking chair surveying her beautiful garden, with the backdrop of the cove and the delightful sapphire blue sea, she thought of how happy she always was to be in a garden. It was her escape from the rigours of life, her solace in times of grief, her peace and quiet away from her demanding youngsters.

She'd never been a knowledgeable gardener, she just planted what she wanted and if it grew, it grew. Some of her gardens had been meticulously planned, some had been functional, some were filled with colour, with others being quite minimalist.

She smiled to herself as she thought back to her very first introduction to the joy of growing and tending plants, and to watching life form out of a sprinkling of tiny seeds placed on damp kitchen roll.

Jenny's mum had always found a way to occupy her children on damp drizzly days. One day, she sat Jenny down at the table, placed a waterproof cloth before her and brought in a collection of items. Jenny couldn't wait to find out what her mum had planned. Firstly, Mum put a little water on an upturned margarine tub lid. Next, she placed a piece of kitchen roll onto the lid, which immediately soaked up the water. She then handed Jenny a small sachet, which had been torn open. She told Jenny to scatter the contents onto the damp kitchen roll. Very carefully Jenny followed her mother's instructions.

"Now we must put this on the windowsill and be patient for a few days," Mother directed.

"Why must we be patient?" asked Jenny.

"Just wait and you will see," her mother suggested.

For the first couple of days there was no change, but then it happened.

Jenny was fascinated by the tiny seeds when each one, in turn, began to split into two tiny green leaves supported on an almost transparent stem. She was mesmerised when, every day, the stalk grew longer and the green leaves grew bigger.

The kitchen paper was a mass of green heads, and Jenny felt a little sad when her mother said she could now cut them and make an egg and cress sandwich. All the care she had put in to it, all the waiting, and then within a second, they were cut down and gone. Mum explained that farmers planted and tended crops every year so they could be harvested for people to eat.

When Jenny was quite small there wasn't a garden at her house, only an old shed and a chicken coop with several hens, which provided the family with fresh eggs, but also to her horror, roast chicken dinners on Sundays! Mum again explained that farmers bred animals which eventually became food items for people to eat. The young Jenny decided there and then, she did not want to become a farmer.

Eventually her father decided to buy a car, so the shed and coop were dismantled to make way for a garage. Yet again there was no room for a garden. Many of her friends lived in houses with gardens and she would dream how, one day, she would have a beautiful garden all of her own.

One day they held a competition at school to plant a sunflower seed and awarded a prize for the tallest flower grown. Jenny had asked her mother to let her have a flower pot, which she filled with compost and carefully planted the black and white seed inside. Each day she watered it, watched it, and then waited, and waited, and waited some more, but nothing appeared.

'Why is nothing growing?' she asked herself, confused.

Jenny asked the other children at school how it was that their seeds were growing, with each of them being eager to tell her how well theirs were growing, however, for Jenny, there were still no signs of life.

She was beginning to despair that it would ever grow, but then one morning she saw a tiny sprout appearing out of the damp compost. No one could have encouraged it more than she did. She talked to it each morning, and as soon as school was over, she went straight back to check how much it had grown. Her father put a stick into the soil and wrapped cotton around the stem of the sunflower, fastening it to the stick to provide support.

Days passed and the tiny head now started to unfold. She didn't care about winning a prize, she was just so in love with the fact that she had grown this beautiful flower.

One day, after rushing home from school, Jenny did her usual trip to look at her treasured bloom. She stood in utter disbelief and horror as she gazed at the flower pot. All that was left was just a tall thin stem with absolutely no flower head. Immediately, tears filled her eyes. How could someone have been so cruel? She didn't ask who had done it, because she didn't really want to know, but all her care and attention growing it had been wasted. She ventured inside and funnily enough, nobody said anything, but they must have noticed her tear stained cheeks.

She went to make her way up to her room, but when passing the hall table, she saw, standing erect in all its splendour and potted in a tall glass, was her beautiful sunflower.

'Why?' she wanted to know. 'Why did no one ask her?'

At the dining table, everyone seemed uncharacteristically quiet. Her brother, Mark, looked guilty, incredibly sheepish, and kept shuffling in his seat.

Mum eventually broke the silence. "Mark brought this for me from the pot outside. He thought I would like it." Her mother talked about his gift as if it was okay that he'd taken Jenny's pride and joy to give to his mother, and get into her good books.

Jenny glared at her brother across the table.

"It's only a flower, for goodness sake," Mark told her ignorantly. Totally lost for words, Jenny sat in silence.

As Jenny remembered this and how upset she'd been, she smiled and recollected as to how many sunflowers she had to cut down in her own garden when harvesting the seeds for cooking with, and making oil.

Returning to her reminiscing, she remembered when Dad came home from work shortly after the sunflower incident, he'd carried a small package under his arm.

"Hey Jenny," he said. "This is for you." Presents were normally only given on birthdays and at Christmas, so Jenny was a little surprised.

She carefully took the box out of the brown paper packaging and saw that the picture on the box was of a lovely garden full of flowers. At first Jenny thought it might be a jigsaw puzzle, but it turned out to be something totally different, something she used and treasured over the years. It was called a miniature garden, and in all the several sections in the box were tiny plants, shrubs and trees; along with small bricks to make walls, borders and miniature picket fences. A large folded board came with the package, and on it were the tiny holes where you could fix the flowers and bushes wherever you would like them, to create a fabulous garden. It could be easily moved and changed to suit your own taste and mood. She added her own garden creations, making a greenhouse and pergola from ice-lolly sticks.

Jenny loved it, although she yearned for the real thing. One day she wanted her own garden space, where she could be creative and have the chance to grow a wide variety of beautiful blooms.

When an allotment eventually came available at the back of their house, Jenny's dad purchased it. He dug vegetable plots and built a large greenhouse, where he grew tomatoes. They really did taste so much better than the ones bought from the supermarket, and the smell that greeted you when you entered the greenhouse, was just truly sensational!

A small triangle of the allotment had been fenced off by the previous owner, and Jenny was delighted when her father announced, "Jenny, I am giving you that area over there. You can have it so you can build, and grow your own garden." She was very excited when hearing this.

She envisaged paths and arches, with rose gardens and herbaceous borders, but the triangle of land was quite small. Because of this, her dreams were affected by the reality of the situation.

Nevertheless she rescued some old red bricks, and in a herringbone style, she formed a path that curved from one side to the other. At the rear of the allotment stood a railway line that carried coal from the pit to the power stations. The track had been raised and built by using the rocks and soil from the coal excavations.

Jenny clambered up and down the steep sides several times, collecting large rocks that were to be her rockery. She lovingly placed these heavy rocks in the corner of the triangle, gradually building the levels almost like a terrace, her grandma called it. Her grandma, a keen gardener herself, brought cuttings and bulbs from her own garden. She loved seeing how happy Jenny was, with her being there in her own little garden.

After winter, when spring began to warm the soil, shoots appeared in the rockery. Strong and healthy daffodils, narcissus and tulips appeared bringing vibrant colours to the little garden. Mum bought her some bedding plants, and Jenny lovingly planted them in summer. When everything was in full bloom, passers-by often remarked at how beautiful the little garden was.

Jenny smiled, remembering how happy she had been in creating this oasis of flowers amidst all the vegetables, potatoes, cauliflowers, peas, onions and carrots.

Over the years, Jenny blossomed into a beautiful young teenager. The garden would eventually take second place in her life and it was passed to her younger sister, who sadly did not have the same dedication as Jenny, resulting in it soon becoming overgrown and neglected.

Jenny smiled as her thoughts now drifted to the garden, to the meadows and orchards at the house where she and husband, John, lived on the moors.

John had taken her to see it one evening. The stars had been shining and the lights of the town below were glistening like a billion lasers in a moonlit sky. He'd asked her if she liked it, and she had thought the house looked beautiful.

John had told her he thought something was missing, but Jenny had thought it perfect. He told her, as he proposed to her that night that it was her that was missing. She knew that she had to live with him, then and there.

There was much work to be done, and over time they completely renovated the cottage and surrounding land. Some of the land was used for stables, some converted into kennels, an area in which to exercise the horses, along with an orchard that provided them with apples, pears and plums.

Jenny had a kitchen garden out at the back of the house where she grew and cultivated herbs. At the front of the house, John made lovely window boxes which Jenny filled with flowers, and they built a herringbone path, just like she had in her first garden, which led to a rustic arch and wooden gate. It was quite the chocolate box cottage to look at.

When the children, Suzie, James and Laura came on the scene, areas were used for swings and slides, with a flat paved area for a paddling pool in the summer.

Just as her mother had shown her the miracle of growing, Jenny taught her children the same lessons. Over time, they too learned to love the miracles of nature.

There was one special corner of the garden that was dedicated to their daughter, Emily. It was her memorial garden.

Emily had been John and Jenny's third child, but sadly she had died quite soon after being born. John and Jenny always said that Emily was, 'A little star that came to earth and had shined for such a short time.'

The little rockery had a stone carved with Emily's name. It had been engraved with a shooting star; just like the one Jenny and John had seen the night when she died.

Jenny took great pleasure in keeping everything just so in the garden. She was forever in the garden, and would be there as soon as it became light in the morning and while the rest of the family slept. She always cherished this quiet time of solitude.

Time flew by. The children were growing up, and John and Jenny had more time for each other.

A holiday to the Greek island of Kos, their first holiday without the children, set their minds thinking. They fell in love with Kefalos and returned many times to holiday there. It felt like a little piece of heaven, so when they decided later to build a house in Kefalos for them to use, firstly as a holiday home, and then as a place of residence when they retired, Jenny was excited to create not only a lovely home, but a different sort of garden in what would be a more mild and a much drier climate.

She planned her dream garden whilst the builders worked on the house, which had fabulous views over the Bay of Kamari, standing high on the hill outside the village.

All plans were scuppered when her husband, John became ill. The two of them had such love for Kefalos and such plans for their future life there, being so excited and looking forward to living together on the island. John made Jenny promise to live out the dream they had of living in Kefalos, should anything happen to him.

On the night when he died, John again insisted she finish the project and move out to Kos to live. He told her that whenever she felt sad or lonely, she was to look to the stars and he would be there.

Jenny never forgot those words and thinking about it now, a tear appeared in her eye. She had loved John so much and was devastated at losing him, but out of respect for him she carried out his dying wishes and moved to the house on the hill and made her home in Kefalos.

On sunny days, she tended the garden with its beautiful bougainvillea bushes, the sweet-smelling jasmine, lavender and mimosa. In the evenings, she would gaze out over the gently lit garden, down the steep road that led to the sea and watch for the stars to appear. This was the time when her thoughts would turn to John and the promise he had made, that he would always be there amongst the stars and looking down upon her, keeping her safe.

Although alone, she never felt lonely. She loved living in Kefalos and would think to herself how perfect it would have been if John had been there with her too.

Jenny never thought she would meet anyone who she could love as much as she had loved John, but she did find love again.

Jenny sighed and shifted herself on the rocking chair. She had met a wonderful Greek man called Yiannis, who like her, had tragically lost his partner. Slowly, they both learned to love again.

They both had wonderful memories of a small cove somewhat secreted by gorse bushes. It was special to them both, so it was here that Yiannis had planned to build their home together. She had not told the children about Yiannis because she was worried that they might see it as disrespect for their father. However, in this respect, she had worried unnecessarily.

Laura, her youngest daughter, had invited Jenny to attend her graduation ceremony in England and Jenny was so excited to be there. The family were surprised when she took Yiannis with her to meet them all. Yiannis told the family of his love for their mother and was readily accepted as part of the family.

When Jenny married Yiannis at the little church on the island of Kastri, James proudly gave his mother away. It had been a great day, full of love and many celebrations.

Jenny and Yiannis had a very happy life together. When Laura was escaping from a bad relationship back in England, she came to stay, and lived at the house on the hill above Kamari bay.

Laura had met a Greek man who changed her life and taught her what real love should be like. His mantra was always, "When the stars align." She had made her home with him when they married, high above the village in a fantastic walled residence.

Not everyone, or everything had been a bed of roses, and Jenny had been there to support her daughter when she had miscarried and suffered terrible depression as a result. No one could have been happier than Jenny herself when, finally, Laura announced that she was expecting Demetris.

The garden, which Jenny now looked out on from her rocking chair, was more minimalist, as the backdrop of the cove and sea could never be outshone.

Deep in her thoughts, Jenny likened her children to the flowers she'd grown, giving them loving tender care, watching them grow and producing offspring.

James, her son, who looked so much like his father and shared his temperament, fell in love and married the girl he met at medical school, a girl named Caitlin, and together the pair became esteemed paediatric doctors. Late in their marriage Caitlin was shocked to discover she was pregnant and she gave birth to a 'Down's Syndrome' girl. They named their daughter, Grace, and both loved her unconditionally.

James had dreamed of living in Kefalos, and his sister wanted nothing more. He continually said if it was 'written in their stars,' then it would happen.

They were given the opportunity to work and live in Kefalos, and they worked together in the village at the paediatric centre funded by Laura's husband, Nikos, where they enjoyed life as part of the wonderful Kefalos community.

Suzie, Jenny's elder daughter, visited Kefalos regularly, although she never dreamed of ever one day moving there. It was however Suzie's daughter, Mia, who came to live and work with her Uncle James at the centre. Mia met and fell in love with Sophia, and they were married on the beach close to where they had met.

Jenny remembered how shocked she was when finding out she was to be a great grandmother, and it had made everyone laugh at the time. Mia and Sophia had announced that they were expecting a baby, and although Jenny was thrilled for them, sadly she was never to meet or hold her great grandchildren.

Jenny was always happy that the majority of her family had moved to Kefalos. She also knew that John would have been happy about it too.

Jenny was growing stiff in her chair, but she felt very happy to be reliving her life with such happy memories. She'd been brave enough to start a new life in Kefalos. She saw how happy her family was here, and was glad she had fulfilled her promise to John when she'd move here. She looked out of the big picture window. This really was the garden of her dreams.

She left the chair and walked down towards the cove, and as she neared the top of the cliff, she saw the bronze body of someone standing on the beach and looking out to sea. Strangely she found that she didn't have to struggle down the steep cliff face as she normally had to. Her descent was like that of an agile youngster almost floating above the ground.

She ran across the beach to where the waiting man beckoned to her. She found herself unsure if it was John or Yiannis, she couldn't quite make it out. However, it didn't matter as they had morphed together and become the same person as far as she was concerned. What puzzled her now was how young and fit he looked standing there before her.

She looked down at her own body and was mystified with what she saw. Gone were the ravages of time. Her figure was once more that of a young woman. She fell easily into his strong arms. They paused for a moment, holding each other tightly. Then, hand in hand, they walked slowly into the sea.

The Greek police found Jenny the next day. She had passed away in her rocking chair on the balcony overlooking the sea. She passed with a massive smile on her face. With no sign of pain, and no sign of fear, Jenny had died happy.

Who knows if Jenny did, or did not see her ever growing family? Maybe from the garden of her dreams in heaven, she looked down with love and admiration, so proud of all their achievements.

CHAPTER 2
ALEXANDER AND ANGELIS

Maisie had met her husband, Damon, through their joint love of horse jumping. Maisie was surprised when she'd learned that Damon was originally from Kefalos, where her grandmother, auntie, uncle and sister now lived. When Damon had inherited a riding school on Kos, he'd asked Maisie to go to live there with him. She was reluctant at first, resulting in Damon moving to Kos alone.

When Maisie discovered she was expecting a child and Damon found out, he asked her to marry him. They eventually married and together, they came to live in Kefalos. Although their son, Alexander, was born in England, he was brought up on the island.

Just like both his parents, Alexander had an affinity for horses even from a very early age. He would carry the empty buckets to the feed room, helping his mum to prepare the daily feeds and make ready for the horses.

He would climb on the fence of the field where the horses grazed and would call to them, loving it when they came to him. They would nuzzle up to him, pressing deeply into his chest and almost knocking him from the fence.

Even in these tender years, he thought nothing of climbing on even the biggest of the horses and rode them bare back, just holding onto a clump of their manes. He would regularly go out on the escorted rides with the tourists along the beaches and paddling in the sea. He had no fear, and as a result of this, the horses trusted him.

Many of the tourists who came to ride at his father's stables fell in love with Alexander as he was such an adorable, cheeky individual. His dark curls grew long and his face was tanned, but it was his incredible laugh that caught everyone's attention. He was always happy and laughing, and when he became a big brother to Angelis, he made it quite clear that he ruled the roost. Little and somewhat fragile, Angelis had to toe the line and always deferred to Alexander. His cousins, Demetris and Toula, always kept a watchful eye on him, just like all the other members of his family.

Alexander loved to go down to the beach at Kamari bay with his parents, and he took great pleasure in feeding the little fish that would appear, splashing and fighting for the crumbs he'd thrown to them on Cavos beach. He loved the chill of the sea and swam each morning. He learned to hunt the squid and octopus under the rocks, being pleased to offer anything he caught to the local restaurants, and they would always reward him with a few euros.

At school, he quickly fitted in. He became friends with many of the children in his age group. However, he was happiest most of all at the riding school, spending practically all his free time there.

Over the years, Alexander went on to run the riding school. His parents took a back seat and began a happy retirement in Kefalos, now able to go to the beach every day for a swim, or to relax together and enjoy coffee in the tavernas.

Angelis was very different from Alexander. Unlike his older brother, he was fair haired and had piercing blue eyes. He was a quiet and contented baby, sleeping often or lying awake, he never made a sound.

Although Alexander tried to play with, and share toys with his little brother, he received little response. Angelis would gather up his toys and place them side by side, becoming upset if Alexander interfered with the arrangement.

As he grew older, he loved to gather pebbles and driftwood from the beach. He would sit quietly in the soft sand, letting it run through his fingers and watching every grain as it fell.

When he went to preschool, he didn't seem to want to mix with his peers, preferring to sit alone. He loved the crayons and paper, and before starting to draw a picture he would lay them all out in a perfect line. The teacher noticed that if there were creases, or marks on any of the art paper, he would not use it, preferring to sort through the pile until he found one that was not damaged in any way.

Because his drawings were intricate and precise, his teacher reported this obsessive behaviour to the psychologist at the paediatrician centre in the village, who spoke to his parents, Maisie and Damon. Once they had been made aware of this behaviour, they watched Angelis more closely and realised there were many things he did that could be considered obsessive.

As time went by, Angelis became more isolated and self-centred. He did not interact with others and flinched at any physical contact. He began the descent into a world of his own. Maisie and Damon were so upset by this. It was dreadful to feel that there was no connection, or relationship between them and their son. In fact, Angelis didn't have a relationship with anyone.

It was decided to refer for him to be tested for autism. The test led to the conclusion that he was indeed quite high up on the spectrum. He was never openly aggressive to others, but he would panic and throw a tantrum and sometimes stop breathing when things didn't go his way. It was frightening for his parents to see this and deal with it. Damon found that music could help to soothe his son when he was upset.

Following a meeting with the staff at school, a specialist teacher was arranged to work with him using music. When certain pieces of music were played, Angelis' pupils could be seen moving slowly from side to side and he would sway to the beat of the music. As he grew older, the outside world was forgotten for him.

When left alone with the music playing, he began to dance his own special dance. He soon became extremely skilled at pirouetting, jumping, and spinning in time to the music.

Maisie and Damon decided to let him go to the local dance school, where he was actually the only boy amongst a large class of young girls. In no time at all he became a very talented dancer, and seemed to forget about the outside world while he danced.

At home, he would put music on in his room and perform complicated dance moves, not caring if anyone was watching him. Maisie and Damon learnt to use music to calm down Angelis' panic attacks and tantrums.

At junior school, some of the more unkind children laughed at him and called him a sissy, but he didn't seem to care. Music took him far away from them and their name calling.

He waited anxiously each week for his visit to the dance school. He was a quick learner, and when the school did a presentation evening, it was Angelis who was chosen to perform major roles, or solos. He received such accolades for his performances, and loved every second of them.

Maisie and Damon were told about a special school in Italy where children like Angelis could be tutored in their preferred topic, whilst being taught by specialist teachers. Much as they didn't want him to go away, it was decided that this opportunity for Angelis to do what he liked best, could not be missed.

They visited their son at the school often, but they received little response from him. His reluctance to be hugged really upset them. They once brought him back to Kefalos, but they soon took him back to Italy, as his anxiety level was more than obvious and he began to self-harm!

Once back at the school, he calmed down and quickly returned to his normal daily routines, continuing to improve his dancing ability and thriving on it.

Years later, Angelis became the principal dancer with a major dance company and performed all over the world. Maisie and Damon could not have been prouder.

CHAPTER 3
KALI & BABIS

Kali had had a happy childhood. There was no stigma attached to the fact that she had two mums rather than the traditional mum and dad. She herself never questioned this, it was how it had always been and she thought herself lucky to have such loving and caring parents.

During the long summer holidays, she played on the island's beaches and swam in the shimmering, crystal clear sea, becoming a very accomplished swimmer at an early age.

Most of the family preferred the long sandy beach at Kochylari to many of the other beaches, but Kali loved to go to Lagada. When there, she would walk in either direction from the beach towards the famous Paradise and Bubble beach, where the sea was like a small Jacuzzi, caused by the air in vents from the volcano on Nisyros breaking through the sandy bed and gently rising to the surface.

Paradise beach was always busy, as many tourists travelled the length and breadth of the island to enjoy this much-discussed stretch of sandy beach, although Kali still preferred Lagada.

Kali walked down the blue and white palette steps that led down to the sandy beach at Lagada. It was still quite early and only the ardent sun worshippers were there at this hour. She wondered sometimes if they had slept on the sun loungers all night, to ensure that when the sun rose they would catch the very first rays and then lie there till dusk.

She chose a sunbed at the end of the row and positioned her towel, securing it with four jumbo pegs to keep it steady in the morning breeze. The wind was constant, being very welcome in the summer to keep you cool. She took her books out of her bag so she could study whilst it was quiet, as her concentration was disturbed when families with screaming youngsters arrived for the day. She smiled as she returned footballs kicked by little boys, which ended up under her sunbed.

The course she was on involved a lot of study, with much of it being distance learning and commitment to the work, so she had to discipline herself to resist the temptation to sit and drink coffee with her friends. Most mornings, she allowed herself to study on the beach and would then treat herself to a bathe in the sea before leaving.

After two hours of reading, the noise levels on the beach had increased significantly, and when she looked up now she saw that most of the sun beds were occupied. She listened to the loud conversations and, being bilingual, could understand English and Greek, and of course the Greeks always spoke loudly, shouting at each other as if they were arguing. She noticed that many tourists looked up to see what the raucous behaviour was about, but when they saw the smiles and heard the laughter of the shouting individuals, they settled back to their sunbathing.

During the summer months, Kali had seen so many battles over sun beds. It amused her greatly when one Greek family attempted to take a mere six foot of another plot rented by another Greek. There were loud accusations of wrongdoings, much pointing of fingers and stamping of feet between the Greeks, who would blow hot and cold. Kali no longer reacted to these debacles.

The sea was cool today but it was invigorating, taking away the stiffness of having sat cross-legged on the sunbed with her books set out before her. Much of the information and work sessions were on her laptop, but she loved the feel of books. She knew if she wanted to get a placement at the local law firm, she would have to gain high grades across all subject areas.

Most of her immediate family were involved with the paediatric centre on the hill above the bay of Kamari. It was funded by her mother's Greek uncle, and managed by her other uncle and was the showpiece of the village, catering for the needs of all children, big and small.

She had herself been admitted there as a young girl when a summer cold had progressed to a serious chest infection, causing her to have difficulty with breathing. Her two mums had panicked and beseeched their Uncle James to help her recover. She had come through the trauma without any lasting problems.

Unlike many of her family members she was not interested in taking up a career in medicine, but had chosen instead the difficult training to become a lawyer. She had enjoyed attending school in the village, and then afterwards at the high school in Antimachia. She liked to study and threw herself wholeheartedly into the gaining of knowledge so she was ready for further training to be able to do the job she wished.

A few years later, she began her career proper when she was recruited by a local law firm.

From the moment Kali's baby brother, Babis, came to live with Mia and Sophia, he was spoilt rotten by his big sister. She loved to rock him in his cradle and feed him his bottle. She enjoyed making him laugh by tickling him, or making him jump by hiding her face and suddenly reappearing and shouting – "Boo!"

As with all members of the extended family, Babis liked to swim in the sea and visit the nearby beaches. As soon as he was capable of riding a bike, he would take himself off down the hill to the harbour, where he would spend long summer days bathing in the sea or fishing off the harbour wall.

Although Kali was his older sister, he always felt as though he had to protect her, especially when at school, as she was much shyer than he was and sometimes she was picked on a little. Kali always called him her special policeman, and Babis loved that she thought of him that way. Maybe this was what steered him to the career he chose.

Ever since he could remember, Babis had always been keen to join the police force when older. To achieve this, he worked hard to get the relevant qualifications he needed.

There would be a recruitment seminar soon and likely recruits were asked to send a letter showing their qualifications, along with their reasons for wanting to join the police force. Babis took the opportunity to put together a CV and covering letter explaining his passion for the work, along with his burning desire to join the force. He read it again, adjusted certain paragraphs and checked his spelling, because he wanted it to be as good as it possibly could be.

Having posted his submission, he tried to relax. There was nothing more he could do; it was now simply a waiting game. He wondered if, and hoped that he had what they were looking for.

Eventually, when he checked at the post office, there was a letter waiting in his mail box addressed to him. He tentatively opened the envelope and smiled as he read the first line of the communication.

'You have been selected to attend a recruitment seminar. This will include both mental and physical tests, personality testing and a presentation by you to show us why you want to become a serving police officer. Following this, you will be required to attend a formal interview with the chief of police.'

The letter went on to advise when and where this appointment would take place, and gave details of the structure of the included events. If successful, he would be required to attend further sessions until a decision was made regarding his suitability to become a member of the police force.

Mia and Sophia waved him off as he left in the taxi to journey to the airport, from where he would then travel on to Athens. Once there, he would regularly update them on his progress and what he'd been doing. The feedback from Babis always seemed very positive.

It seemed like an eternity before he returned, telling them he had been asked to go back in a week for further testing. Mia and Sophia were delighted when hearing this, although they felt anxious when waiting for his return at the end of the next week.

They met him at the airport upon his return from his further testing, and both Mia and Sophia were eager to hear the results. He came through the arrivals with hunched shoulders and avoided eye contact. They didn't dare ask how he'd gone on. Looking downtrodden and dejected, he told them that the police chief had decided against recruiting him.

They could tell he was very upset by this decision and sought to comfort him, but he would have nothing of it. He became short tempered and rude, which was totally out of character for him.

Over the coming days, he spent hours inside on his computer and spoke little to anyone. Mia and Sophia were very concerned. They wondered if there was any way they could appeal the decision, but when they suggested this to him, he simply told them not to interfere.

"Just leave it, please," he'd demanded.

Babis finally said he wanted to take a break from Kefalos. He planned to visit somewhere else, although he didn't know where as yet. Mia and Sophia naturally felt heartbroken by this news.

Mia sat deep in thought on Kochylari beach. The wind was extremely strong today and it blew her long dark hair all across her face. She shook her head several times to remove it from in front of her vision, but no sooner had she moved it, then the next gust of wind blew it back across her face again. Eventually she gave up and searched in her bag for a Scrunchie, which, after finding, she used it to secure it tightly on top of her head. She sat facing the sea and rested her head on her upturned arms and remained deep in thought.

Her favourite beach had no joy for her today. Nothing would help her to snap out of her deep depression. Tears welled up in her eyes and trickled down her face. Even though the wind made her salty tears sting, she let them flow freely. There was no one here to see her despair. Her once tranquil, content family life had been in turmoil. She now wondered how she would be able to go on. This was soul destroying.

She thought back to the time when she had first met Sophia, and how she had immediately formed a special relationship with her. She had struggled to come to terms with her feelings at the time, and she had asked her Auntie Laura for help. She'd told Laura how she loved Sophia in a way that she'd never loved any boy.

Mia had been surprised how her relationship was accepted so easily by her aunt, who prompted her to tell her mother, whom she found was equally happy that her daughter had found love and happiness with someone, even if it was with a girl and not a boy.

When all the family came together to welcome Sophia to the fold, Mia learned the importance of true family love, although there had been some confusion for Sophia's parents about the relationship, but they also seemed to come to terms with it over time.

Mia and Sophia had married on the beach close to where they'd met, and began a happy life together in the little house close to the sea. Both of them had wanted children, and with the help of a clinic in Athens, they were delighted to conceive and give birth to their beautiful daughter Kali. Their happiness was completed when a little later, with the help of Mia's Uncle James, they were able to adopt an abandoned baby, and he became their much-loved son, Babis.

Life had been good to them and Mia and Sophia spent special time with their children, watching them grow into two beautiful young adolescents. Mia now longed for those carefree special times. She remembered how she'd been so proud of her children, and Sophia felt exactly the same way.

They were blessed and privileged to have been given the opportunity to be parents to these wonderful children, but it now all seemed to be falling apart. In Mia's mind, it seemed that nothing could be done to return to those wonderful days.

As an adult, neither Mia nor Sophia could prevent Babis from leaving. His discontent at being there in Kefalos was more than apparent. He seemed to always be in a ferociously bad mood, both with himself and with his mothers. It was desperately hurtful for them to see their son like this.

He told them he wanted to be out of there as soon as possible, and once he had found somewhere, he was off in search of a new life. However, whilst he was deciding where he might go, a very surprising event happened.

There was a knock on the front door and Mia went to investigate. She found a woman standing there before her, a scruffy looking woman with messy hair and an unkempt appearance, waiting on her and Sophia's doorstep.

"Can I help you?" Mia asked in Greek, for it was obvious to her that this was a Greek woman. The woman looked a little older than Mia, and had dark circles under her eyes.

She stared directly at Mia and quite gruffly, she bluntly told her, "You have my boy!"

"Sorry, I don't understand," retorted a surprised, Mia.

"My boy," the woman said again. "You have my boy!"

Sophia came to see what all the commotion was about and the three of them continued to speak together in Greek. Sophia held her hands open in despair, as the woman 'became more and more agitated.

"Who told you it was your boy?" demanded Sophia.

"I know! I see you with him! He is my son, Michalis!" the Greek woman argued.

"He's called Babis, and he is our son," Mia retaliated.

"How can this be your son? You are two girls," the woman said hurtfully. "Two girls with a boy, this is not normal! He was given to you at the hospital by another Englishman. I believe this man was from your family. You do this thing to me! You take my child away from me! You steal my child! You stole my beautiful baby and I want him back!"

"Now you hang on a minute," Sophia cried, getting exceedingly angry now. "You abandoned your child many, many years ago, and if Babis was your child, which I doubt very much, he is our son now and has been for all of his life!"

"No, he is mine," the Greek woman again protested.

Babis returned home at that precise moment, and quickly became embroiled in the altercation. "What on earth is going on here?" he queried, but was quickly shushed by his two mothers.

After a while the woman seemed to calm down. Although neither Mia nor Sophia wanted to agree to it, Babis suggested he should go for a walk with the woman to talk with her and hopefully try to settle the argument.

As they left the house Mia burst into tears. "This can't be happening," she wept. "We cannot agree to her having him after all this time."

"We need to speak to someone," Sophia suggested.

"I need to speak to James. Maybe he can speak with the authorities and sort this out," Mia said, by now in floods of tears.

"Where is she?" Sophia questioned as soon as Babis returned.

"She's gone, Mum," Babis replied.

Upon hearing this, Mia immediately phoned her uncle, James. Still sobbing, she related to him what had just happened.

"Slow down, Mia, tell me again," Uncle James said calmly. "How did this woman know where you lived, and why is she so adamant that Babis is her son and not yours?"

Mia tried to explain, but it seemed nothing could be done. Babis was legally their son, but this woman claimed to be his birth mother. They didn't know what to do. However, both Mia and Sophia, and even Uncle James were all shocked when it was Babis who finally came to the decision.

"After speaking to the woman, I have decided to go and live with her at her home on the island," he announced somewhat heartlessly. "I feel I owe it to her to get to know her a little better." Again, Mia and Sophia were heartbroken.

Although they were unhappy with their son's decision to spend this time with his birth mother, they had to agree that the explanation of why he wanted to do this showed that he'd carefully thought it through.

He emphasised that at the present time he felt lost, having been rejected for the job with the police, a job which he'd wanted all of his life. In his depressed state, he couldn't see any road forward.

Maybe finding out about his real family and why his birth mother had abandoned him at the paediatric centre all those years ago, might help him to come to terms with things.

There was a degree of urgency about Babis wanting to go with his birth mother that was quite upsetting for Mia and Sophia. He had always been their pride and joy, and they loved him very much. Even in their distress at his leaving, they were willing to let go and to allow him to follow what he thought was the best course of action for him.

Babis insisted on only taking the minimum of his things with him, since he told his mums that he intended to return home in the not too distant future. It was hurtful that he didn't pack a lot of his more personal possessions, as Mia and Sophia thought these would have been reminders of his time with them.

Farewells were said and hugs were given. Holding back the tears, the mums waved as Babis stepped into a waiting car. They had no idea exactly where he was going, but he promised to let them know as soon as he was settled there.

The two mums turned to each other and found solace in each other's arms, now freely letting the tears flow unchecked.

Over the coming months, Mia and Sophia caught sight of Babis from a distance, although they were unable to catch his eye as he moved away. He was surrounded by a crowd of younger men. They noticed how he'd let his hair grow longer, and he also looked a little slimmer than when they'd last set eyes on him.

Oh, how they missed him. With no phone calls or messages from their son, they had no idea where he was living. They just prayed he was okay and that one day he would get back in touch, although they had a long wait ahead of them.

Mia hadn't heard from, or seen Babis for some time, so when the phone rang, he was the last person she was expecting it to be.

"Hi, how are you?" she asked, but she did not receive a reply. There was a pregnant pause, but then Babis spoke.

"I need your help," he said speaking softly, as though slightly embarrassed. "I'm in a bit of trouble financially. Could you possibly pay some money into a mate's account?"

"Of course," Mia commented, but then questioned her son. "Whatever is the matter?"

"I can't talk about it at the moment," Babis quickly and bluntly replied.

"Okay. Well how much do you need?" Mia asked, now almost in tears.

"I could do with five hundred euros," pleaded Babis.

"That's a lot of money" Mia replied, quite shocked at the amount.

"Look, if you can't do it, just say so and I won't bother you again," Babis shouted, both sharply and rudely. This was so unlike him. He'd always spoken to Mia with great respect before.

"I didn't say I couldn't do it," Mia told him.

"I'm sorry to ask you, and I'll explain soon, but can you pay it into this account?" As he said this, Babis gave her the bank details she'd require.

"Okay, I will do it now," Mia stated.

"Thanks," he replied, but not at all thankfully, or so it seemed to Mia.

"Well, how are you?" Mia questioned.

Immediately the line went dead. He had ended the call with no niceties or explanations. All sorts of things ran through her head, but she thought it must have been urgent for him to ask.

Mia went onto her mobile banking app and did the transaction. She tried to message Babis to tell him she had completed the transfer, but the number was blocked. She would have to tell Sophia when she got home, but then wondered if it was best to say nothing, as it would upset her.

Weeks passed and she never heard from Babis again. Mia wondered where and how he was. Her heart ached to think that he was in some sort of trouble. That hurt increased threefold when the next contact eventually came from him.

"It's me," was the opening line from Babis. His voice was gruff and guttural. Mia had to take a deep breath to compose herself. "Can you hear me?" her son queried curtly.

"Yes" she managed to reply.

"Look, I need money. Can you help or not?" he asked sharply.

"Of course," Mia stated.

"I need five hundred," Babis ordered. "Can you do it soon? I can't say anything else, I have someone with me. Can you do it now?"

"Well, yes," she said with tears in her eyes. How could he treat her like this?

"Okay, do it now. Send the money to the same account as last time." Once again the line immediately went dead. No please - No thank you – Nothing!

Without a second of hesitation, Mia sent the money to the account as specified before. She loved her son so much and she would always help, but she wished she knew what was happening.

After this, there was a period of time without any contact, but then a call came through again from Babis.

"This isn't my phone," he began, "so don't try to call me back or text me. I'm going away for a while. Can I have one hundred euros for my ticket?"

Having spoken to Sophia about the situation after the earlier request, they had agreed that if their son needed something, they would always support him. Because of this, they both agreed they would always help him financially because they loved, and missed him so much, although it was still heartbreaking for them.

They had so many questions which they wanted to ask, but the opportunity never arose. All phone calls were cut short by Babis, and sadly they had no way of getting back in touch. They tried to come to terms with the fact that their son no longer wanted to live with them, but they never gave up hope that one day he might change his mind and return.

CHAPTER 4
THE TRAIL BEGINS

Mia and Sophia sat with Kali outside Corner Café. It had been several months since they had seen Babis, and then he'd ignored them as he was with a group of Greek boys. All three of them missed him terribly.

His room was still just as he'd left it. Letting him go to his natural mother had been such a wrench, and had left a large hole in all their hearts.

Kali had now grown into a real beauty, and always caught the eye of the young Greek boys. However, her priority was, and had always been her career. She worked hard at her studies, and in a sense, was a perfect daughter.

She worried about her two mothers, who in turn were always worrying about Babis, ever since they'd been told that his birth mother drifted from job to job, and place to place. They often wondered if he was eating properly, as he looked very underweight when they last saw him last. He also looked somewhat dishevelled and had dark circles round his eyes, although to Mia and Sophia, they were still such beautiful eyes, but maybe they were biased.

The two had tried to let him go, but in their hearts, they never would. He'd only been days old when they first saw him, and only weeks old when he'd come to live with them. His adoption had taken a while, but helped by Uncle James and his high standing within the community, it eventually came through. The girls had been overjoyed when Babis legally became their son.

A few more months had passed by and still they had not seen, or heard from him. They tried to rationalise it. This was how it would be now. He was a grown man, who could make his own choices in life, but he was still their son, and he always would be.

As they sat in front of Corner Cafe they spotted an ambulance making its way towards the harbour. The girls noticed its blue lights were flashing. Shortly after, it was followed by a police car, also with flashing blue lights. They wondered what might have happened, perhaps there'd been some trouble in the water off the bay, or perhaps an accident involving a car, or a quad bike had overturned. They were shocked when they saw the coroners van coming along the road.

"Someone must have died," Sophia muttered to Mia.

They didn't think about it any further until the local gossip got back to them. Apparently an old woman had been found by locals, dead on the harbour. The rumour being spread suggested that the woman was a drug addict who had overdosed. They listened, but took it all with a pinch of salt, as rumours were always exaggerated by the locals, but then the gossip became more frightening for them.

"What a shame her son was in prison," said one young man.

"Maybe this is what made her do it," another young man, his friend said, adding to the tale.

"Someone said the son was called, Babis," the first of the two revealed.

Mia's ears pricked up when hearing this. She had heard rumours about his birth mother's reputation, but hadn't really connected her to the death in the harbour until she heard the name, Babis.

Could it be? No -It couldn't possibly be true, surely not. Had their son, Babis, been in prison? Surely not!

Her head pounded as she tried to make sense of what was being said about their beloved adopted son. Sophia questioned the locals about this story they were hearing, trying to find out if it was truth or rumour about the dead woman's son, and if it really was their Babis that they were speaking about.

It was like being caught in a nightmare, from which they couldn't wake up. They gleaned as much information as they could and tried to assimilate it and put it into perspective. One person had said it was the son's fault that the mother had died. Another said the woman had always been in trouble, even as a teenager. It seemed that history was repeating itself, with her boy seemingly heading the same way. Others said he used to be such a nice boy until he went to high school and got in with a bad crowd. Others said he had been caught stealing and drug dealing.

Sophia and Mia walked along in silence, but all the time deep in thought, trying to deal with everything they'd heard.

"How do we discover the truth?" Mia finally asked.

"How will Kali feel about this?" Sophia responded. "She'd always been really close to Babis, and they played happily together throughout their childhood. I wonder if Nikos or James will know anything."

"I don't know who to ask to find out what has really happened," Mia sighed, although she decided to phone her uncle.

Even though he was no longer very active at the paediatric centre, Mia's Uncle James was still a respected member of the community and could perhaps help in finding something for them.

He was shocked to hear the stories and said he would immediately contact a friend who worked at the police station in Antimachia.

"I will also speak to the coroner's office regarding the dead woman to see if she has been formally identified," he offered to the girls.

Mia and Sophia waited with bated breath for James to get back to them. When he did, he confirmed that the dead woman was indeed the birth mother of Babis, and told the girls that it was to be announced on the local news later. Apparently she had died from a drug overdose and had been found propped up against the rocks in the harbour.

Official records had shown that she had no next of kin. It would seem that she'd failed to have the adoption rescinded. Finding any information was proving difficult, with the police at Antimachia having no knowledge of any arrests. For this reason they could offer no help whatsoever.

Sophia and Mia were mortified to think that Babis could be anywhere. More importantly, if what they'd heard was true, their son could even be in prison! Nikos tried to pull some strings to gain more information, but the days passed with them hearing nothing. They had spoken to the coroner's office, where it was confirmed that they were prepared to pay for the funeral of the birth mother of Babis.

James told them he'd discovered that Babis may be brought back to Kefalos by the authorities, so he could be present at his mother's funeral. Mia and Sophia had thought they would attend out of respect. They also had the idea that they might be able to find some information about their son.

When the day arrived for the funeral, they were the only ones at the graveside. It saddened them to think that this was the poor woman who'd given them such a precious and special gift, all those years ago.

Sophie and Mia searched the cemetery, but saw no one else in attendance. They waited for the priest to complete the service, and then turned away from the grave to see a young man standing there, half hidden in the bushes just outside the cemetery. He was dressed in shabby clothing, with dishevelled and greasy hair.

The scruffy man held his hands in front of him, as though shielding his face. When Mia saw the young man, she cried out in horror when she spotted he was wearing handcuffs! A tall man was standing behind him wearing a smart suit – that of a prison warder!

Surely this couldn't be their son, Babis; he was so thin and scruffy. As they walked towards the entrance of the cemetery, the tall prison officer put his hand on the shoulder of the young man and he looked across at Mia and Sophia, but then lowered his head.

The officer began to lead Babis towards the waiting vehicle, but in their eagerness to verify if it was their son or not, Mia and Sophia hurried towards the car. However, the driver got out of the vehicle and motioned for them to stay away.

With one last pleading look over his shoulder, Babis was placed in the rear seat of the car, his head being lowered by the tall man to prevent him from accidentally hitting it on the door frame and he was gone. Then the two mothers watched as if in slow motion, as the car was driven away.

Sophia and Mia looked at each other with tears streaming down their faces. Just what was happening to their son, they couldn't comprehend. They loved him and missed him so much.

Heartbroken, they walked back to their car and drove up to their home on the hill, overlooking the Bay of Kamari. Even the sun didn't cheer them up today. The sky didn't seem so blue, and even the sea looked dark, menacing, and uninviting. They needed to know who those men were, and why were they taking Babis away and to where. Who could they turn to? They needed answers.

Mia and Sophia drove to the police station at Antimachia. They journeyed there to see if the staff there could help in tracking down Babis, but they knew nothing about him and could not confirm whether or not he'd been arrested on the island.

One of the men telephoned the main police station in Kos Town to ask if they had any information, but again they drew a blank.

The girls returned home feeling very despondent about the police not being able to provide any information to help them, but they decided they would never give up.

They tried again in the village in Kefalos, searching in the bars and tavernas around the resort. They visited virtually every taverna, from Faros at the harbour, all the way to Katarina's fish restaurant past Ikos, but with no luck.

Friends there sympathised with them but confessed that it was sometime since they had last seen Babis, even though in the past he'd been a regular visitor.

There had been talk in the village and someone had been heard to say they thought that Babis might have gone to Nisyros. The girls, taking no chances, planned a trip to go there and investigate.

They drove to Kardamena and caught the ferry that went directly to the port at Mandraki. The sea was quite calm so the trip took less than an hour. When they arrived, they walked from the harbour into the village. The last time they'd come here it had been on a pleasure trip taken on Nikos' yacht. Today however brought them no pleasure whatsoever.

Sophia had been told that Babis and some other young men had been seen in one of the tavernas along the sea front. Clasping their most recent photograph of their son they went in and out of every shop and taverna, asking if anyone had seen him. It certainly wasn't comforting for them when each shopkeeper or taverna owner shook their heads, saying they had never seen him. Mia reminded them that he had grown his hair since the photograph was taken and had also lost weight, but still the answer was the same. "No, I'm sorry, I have not seen him."

They decided to eat lunch and then continue their task of trying to find their son. Whilst eating the food, a young waiter approached. "Can I see the photograph please?" he requested.

"Of course," Mia said, offering the picture to him. "Do you recognise him? Have you seen him recently?"

"You say his hair is longer?" the waiter questioned, taking a closer look.

"Yes it is," Sophia replied. "And he is scruffier looking since this picture was taken."

"I think he was with some youths in Emporios, early this morning," the waiter revealed.

Both women jumped up from their seats when hearing this. Leaving the remains of their lunch, they threw some money on the table and thanked the waiter profusely before rushing to find a taxi that would take them to the village of Emporios.

The narrow streets of Emporios were like a rabbit warren and they scoured every one of them, including dead ends and very narrow passageways.

"Have you seen this man?" Mia asked.

"Please look at this picture," pleaded Sophia. "Have you seen this man?"

They showed the photo and asked anyone they came into contact with, as to whether they had seen Babis with a group of young men.

"I'm not certain, but....." one youngster said.

"It could be him," his friend added.

The two young boys told them, although they couldn't be certain, but they thought it was him at one of the viewpoints where you could see the volcano. They had seen him sitting on a wall looking towards the volcano. He looked to be seemingly deep in thought, but he was alone.

Mia and Sophia wandered through the streets of Emporios, continuing to ask anyone they passed if they had seen Babis, showing them the photograph which, to Mia and Sophia, held memories of much happier times.

"Maybe he's been there. It could have been him, but I couldn't really say for sure," one guy said, and the girls thanked him anyway.

They were feeling really disheartened as they travelled back to the harbour in silence. They were worn out, both physically and emotionally. Before they boarded the ferry, they asked the question to the fishermen sitting on their little boats. Many of them just replied by shaking their heads and saying, "No," in answer to this question.

"I am sure I saw him boarding a ferry to Rhodes," a Greek man said, offering a glimmer of hope.

"Can you tell me when?" Mia pleaded.

"It was about an hour ago," the man continued. "He had a black backpack and seemed to be looking around all the time, as if someone might be watching or following him."

Mia and Sophia thanked the man and then travelled back on the homeward bound ferry. During the journey, they were already planning their trip to Rhodes. This had to be taken as soon as possible. It was the best lead they had been given so far.

They spoke to Nikos that night. "Of course I will take you on the yacht," he'd reassured them. However, they surprised him by saying that they wanted to travel to Rhodes on the regular ferry, because they wanted to ask the passengers onboard if they had seen Babis.

"Good idea," Nikos responded, agreeing with the girls reasoning.

Two days later, they caught the early morning ferry to Rhodes. It was a regular crossing for residents of Kos who would go to Rhodes for doctors' appointments, or to visit people in hospitals there. Not all medical appointments could be made on the island of Kos, so people had to travel to Rhodes or even to Athens. Many women would go there for antenatal care and to have their babies.

Once Sophia and Mia were on the ferry, they walked up and down the boat asking everyone whether they had seen this man, and showing them the now battered photo of their son.

"Maybe you have spotted him on another ferry crossing you may have taken," Mia suggested hopefully. However, this continually drew a blank!

As they left the boat, Sophia asked the question again at the shipping office, but, once again they couldn't recall seeing him.

The two caught the bus to Lindos, the place where the fisherman said he thought Babis might be heading. They asked as many people as they could during the time they had there, but kept receiving negative reactions.

Eventually they decided to take a taxi back to the harbour. They didn't care about the cost, as they were tired and weary. They had to concede that the trip had been a complete waste of time, and they despaired of ever finding their son, Babis. Where on earth could he be?

It was early in the morning when the two of them took a gentle stroll along the sea front. There were some early bathers in the sea, along with ardent sun worshippers already taking their places on the sun loungers.

They called into 'Sunlight' and each enjoyed a strong coffee and a chat with Chrisoula, who was always happy to see them. She asked about their progress, but sadly they had nothing to tell her.

"He will find Babis for you. Just ask him," Chrisoula said, pointing heavenward. Sophia nodded, whilst Mia just smiled.

Mia had never been particularly religious, but since they'd not had any joy in finding Babis, she thought she may as well just try a prayer or two.

They continued on with their walk towards the harbour. By now, Cavos beach was beginning to fill and children were already dipping their toes tentatively into the cold sea, before running back to their mums when the waves covered their freezing feet! Mia and Sophia smiled at this spectacle. They were both remembering how they had brought Kali and Babis here to enjoy the shallow waters of the bay.

There was a large cement ship in at the harbour, and as they walked the full length of the pier, they saw some of the workers having a frappé near the boat. Maybe it was worth asking them if they had seen Babis, the girls thought.

Sophia walked over and began talking to the men. At first there was no positive response from any of them, but then one guy came forward.

"I think that maybe on a previous return journey to Athens, a man looking very much like this one in the photograph had hitched a lift onboard, but I cannot be sure," he said, but then added. "He was very quiet and kept his head down for the entire journey. It looked as if he didn't want to be seen or recognised, and he didn't talk to anyone. He was off the ship as soon as we docked. I have no idea where he was heading, and I haven't seen him since."

Although they thanked the man for the information he; provided, once again any hopes for the girls had been dashed!

CHAPTER 5
A MANCHESTER SURPRISE

The women tried to get on with their lives by throwing themselves into their work, but nothing could stop the yearning they had to find Babis. They missed him so much and wondered what could possibly have happened to him. Each and every day, they were reminded of his absence.

Opening a drawer, they noticed there was something there, something that belonged to him; the hedge that he always trimmed for them was growing wild. They had no enthusiasm to do the things that they normally enjoyed. Family gatherings only hurt them, as Babis was often the only relative missing.

There was no laughter anymore, even their own usually affectionate relationship, was suffering too. They wondered if they should give up on their quest. It was constantly dragging them down, with the failure to discover anything at all playing heavily on their hearts.

As usual, they called in at the post office that day to check their mailbox. There was the electricity bill and a reminder that payment for the mailbox was due, but there was also an envelope addressed to both of them. They opened it, and inside the message read -

'If you care about Babis, stop trying to find him. If not, you could lose him forever.'

Mia and Sophia looked at each other in silence, not knowing what to say or how to react. Who could be so cruel as to send this, or was it some kind of joke? When they looked at the envelope it had a Manchester postmark on it. Who in Manchester would send them a letter like this? Again, they were overcome with the desire to discover the culprit at any cost.

Their next decision was to go to Manchester, back to their family roots, and show this letter to the police.

As soon as they could, they arranged flights to Manchester. They were really thankful that they both worked for family, who were happy to let them have the time off to try and find their son. The family had been worried at how badly Mia and Sophia had been affected by the situation with Babis, and were happy to help in any way they could.

When they arrived at Manchester Airport, having only cabin luggage, they went straight through passport control and out onto the concourse. A placard held high above the heads of the scurrying crowd showed them that a lift that had been arranged for them. Mia's cousin was standing there waiting for them.

They had met many years ago at a family event, but they hadn't seen each other since they were teenagers. Mia's cousin, David, also had family of his own, two sons and a daughter, so he knew how hard this was for her and Sophia.

Mia had already explained why they were coming, and David was keen to help them as much as possible. Whilst they travelled from the airport to the hotel, which Mia had booked in advance, they reminisced about their childhood days. David was keen to learn about where they lived, and the life they lived there.

"I will return to collect you tomorrow, and take you both to the police station," David promised, dropping them at their hotel destination.

"Please don't forget we have an appointment at the station," Mia said.

"Of course," David agreed. "Don't worry. I'll get you there on time."

Early the next morning, Mia and Sophia rose, took breakfast, and readied each other for the day ahead. Feeling really nervous about the upcoming meeting, they gathered all the information they had, regarding possible sightings and the letter with the Manchester postmark.

As promised, David arrived at the hotel to take them to the police headquarters. They'd arranged to meet with a 'Sergeant Fry' when there. Arriving at the reception, they told the desk clerk they had an appointment with Sergeant Fry. The clerk looked at them questioningly and then down at his appointment sheet. He looked back up at the two women.

"Just one minute please. I will check if the sergeant is in his office," he said, leaving Mia and Sophia standing nervously in reception. They wondered if there had been a mistake about their appointment. It would be most upsetting to have come all this way for nothing.

The desk clerk returned and guided them through the double doors behind reception and along a long corridor into a large empty board room. He offered them coffee, which they both declined.

A few minutes later, a suited man entered the room. Mia stood and offered to shake the man's hand. "Good morning Sergeant Fry. It really is so very kind of you to see us," she said.

"Not at all, Madam," he smiled, shaking her by the hand and then also offering it to Sophia. He then said something which surprised them.

"Firstly, may I say that I am not Sergeant Fry, but I will explain later why it's me here today talking to you and not the Sergeant."

Mia and Sophia nodded in acceptance of this, although they said nothing. This officer did not offer his name to them, but he did ask them to tell him everything they knew, right from the very beginning.

Mia began to recount the story of them adopting Babis after he had been abandoned by his birth mother, and how he'd been a welcome brother to their daughter Kali. He had been a remarkable toddler, walking and talking early and forever asking questions.

He loved to read and once he had exhausted the children's books available to him he progressed to more adult literature, much preferring the detective or forensic stories. His desire to be a policeman was what drove him on at school, where he'd been an excellent student.

He had grown to be a mature adolescent, with many friends within the Greek community of Kefalos. However, when he was rejected by the police force, it affected him badly and he lost his way.

When his birth mother arrived to ask for him back, Sophia and Mia had been beside themselves with grief, not wanting to let him go, but in their hearts they knew this was his real mother, and for whatever reason she'd abandoned him at birth, she was still related by blood and therefore, tearfully, they had agreed to let him go to live with his mother.

From time to time they caught a glimpse of him, but as time went on they saw him less and less and were told that both mother and son had moved away, but they were never sure where.

Mia told the officer how Babis had contacted them asking for money on a few occasions, but he never gave them a chance to ask how or where he was.

It had come as a great shock to them when they discovered that the woman found dead at the harbour was in fact Babis' mother. Rumours started about how she was a drug addict, her son had also followed her down that road, and drug abuse was responsible for her death.

Tears streamed down Mia's face as she told how they had seen him at his mother's funeral, but how shocked they were that he was in handcuffs. They loved him dearly as their own son, and his character had been such that Mia could never have imagined the path he had taken since being taken away from her and Sophia.

She went on to say how they had tried in vain to find him after this, but all leads they'd been given were worthless. She finished by saying this was what had led them here today, as she pushed the pile of documents across the table to the officer.

"We have recorded as much as we could remember," she told the man who listened intently. "We just need to find out what has happened to our son."

"I understand this and wish I could..." he stopped, seeing how Mia's shoulders had dropped and how disappointed both she and Sophia looked.

"So, what can we do to find him?" Sophia questioned.

"Can I ask you to return tomorrow when my colleagues will be here?" the officer asked. "Then we will see if they can unravel things a little better?"

"Any help at all would be much appreciated," Mia offered.

"We are both at our wits end," Sophia added. As she said this the man stood, indicating that the interview was over.

"Well thank you Mister.....?" Sophia said, but the man just offered his hand and again didn't give his name, as he escorted them back along the corridor and into reception.

"These ladies will be returning tomorrow morning," he said to the desk clerk, and then looking at Mia and Sophia, he suggested, "Shall we say ten-thirty?"

The two both nodded, but in truth were totally bewildered at what had happened today, although both with the hope that something might be brought forward tomorrow.

They returned to their hotel a little deflated. They really had thought that they would discover some answers today, but had become accustomed to disappointment regarding Babis.

"There was something strange about today's visit," Sophia remarked.

"Yes, I thought that," Mia agreed, "not giving his name and saying nothing. Not even asking us more questions. Do you think he was hiding something?"

"I don't know, but it just didn't feel right," Sophia sighed.

"Well tomorrow we will ask more questions," Mia suggested.

"And this time, demand answers!" Sophia stated firmly.

"Well tomorrow is another day," said Mia. "I suggest we get a good night's sleep and be ready to do battle tomorrow."

When they arrived at the police station the next morning they were fired up and ready to do battle, determined to get some answers to their questions. It was a different desk clerk on duty this morning.

"We have an appointment at ten-thirty," Sophia announced stepping forward.

"And who is the appointment with?" questioned the desk clerk.

"I'm not sure," Mia admitted. "We came yesterday and were asked to come back today."

"I have no appointments listed for today, so unless you know who it's with, I can't help you," the man on the desk said, closing the appointment book.

"We came to see Sergeant Fry yesterday," Mia told him.

The desk clerk smiled sarcastically. "Good try," he said. "We don't have any Sergeant Fry." Sophia began to speak, but was again cut off. "I must ask you to leave," the clerk said, interrupting her.

"But we have come all the way from Greece," pleaded Mia.

"Really, but without an appointment, I must ask you to leave." he repeated.

"Maybe you could check again for us. It's very important," Mia asked, raising her voice just a little. The desk clerk looked at them, quite annoyed that they weren't leaving.

"It isn't my job to check. We have about a hundred people working here in the building now. Sorry," he said, although unapologetically.

At that moment, the door behind the clerk opened and out walked the same man they'd seen yesterday. He addressed himself to the clerk.

"What seems to be the problem?" he questioned the younger man.

"They don't have an appointment, Sir, and they don't know who it was they saw yesterday," he replied.

"Well, it was me they spoke with and I didn't give them my name, so the fault is mine, not theirs. I think an apology is required from you," he said, reprimanding the young man.

Without making eye contact, the desk clerk mumbled "Sorry."

Mia and Sophia were then ushered in through the double doors and along the corridor. This time they were taken up a flight of stairs and into another board room. When they entered this room, they saw there were already two other men waiting for them inside.

"Firstly, I must apologise for not giving my name to you yesterday," the first man began. "We try not to disclose our names in this department unless it's absolutely necessary. All three of us work in senior positions in the Undercover Unit here in Manchester. I am known as John and I'm stationed here. This is Patrick," John revealed, whilst pointing to the first of two men, "who has come up from London, whilst Manolis here is from Athens."

Each man nodded as they were introduced, as John continued. "May we use your first names, if you don't mind? It's Mia and Sophia, isn't it?"

The two women nodded in agreement, even though they were feeling a little intimidated at meeting all these high-ranking individuals. What on earth had Babis done to deserve their intervention?

"Okay," John said. "I would like to begin by congratulating you on your perseverance in trying to find your son. You managed to crack a lot of the blocks and red herrings that were put in place to stop you." Mia and Sophia couldn't believe what they were hearing, but continued to listen as John carried on with the discussion. "Fortunately, we were able to slow you down until our work was complete," he said.

"Your work?" questioned Mia.

"Complete?" Sophia added.

"I have to tell you that for all this time, your son, Babis, has been working for us," he said, making both Sophia and Mia looking totally gobsmacked, amazed and dumbstruck!

"I thought he'd failed the interview to join the police?" Sophia was the first to ask.

"That was part of the plan. We wanted everyone to believe that," John revealed. "We recruited him to our undercover department." This was beyond comprehension for the two women.

"So, do you know where he is?" Mia asked nervously.

"Yes, of course we do, but we wanted to ensure the campaign had been brought to a conclusion before he was released from his undercover duties," John confided.

"Hello ladies. My name is Patrick," the second of the Englishmen said. "Your son, Babis has performed a fantastic service for us. You should be very proud of what he has achieved.

He will soon be able to move back to Kos with a role within the police force there on the island. He will never be able to tell you everything he's been doing for the past year or so, but we will allow him to tell you a little, enough at least to put your minds at rest.

We are very grateful for what he has done and we can only offer our sincere apologises for what you two and your family have been through."

Not for the first time since they'd entered the room, Mia and Sophia were flabbergasted! They just couldn't find any words to say.

"We would like to take you both to a venue nearby and there you will learn the exact details, if that is okay with you?" the Greek man, Manolis, offered, joining in with the conversation. Mia and Sophia just nodded in agreement.

They were taken to the back of the building and into a waiting car. John travelled with them and Patrick, whilst Manolis followed in another car. The ride was a short one and the car soon pulled up outside what looked like a country hotel. After leaving the cars, they went inside and walked through to a room found at the back of the building.

"Would you please excuse me for a few moments, ladies?" John requested as he left them in the room. Several minutes later, the door opened and in walked Babis.

Mia and Sophia were elated. They jumped up from their seats and ran to embrace their son. They said nothing, as neither could find the words, with their sheer joy at seeing him being quite overwhelming.

Babis told them to sit down and he sat between them. They each took hold of one of Babis' hands, squeezing them tightly in case he disappeared again. They had so many questions raging through their heads, but for the moment they could only sit in silence.

Babis took a deep breath, wondering if they would ever understand what he had done and been through. After a few moments of silence, he eventually spoke.

"Please believe me when I say, I can tell you very little about where I have been, and why." He stopped and looked at his two mothers who were clinging on to his every word. "Please let me begin by saying how much it has grieved me to hurt you two and Kali. Maybe one day you will understand." Babis went quiet, as if retracing the steps and events in his mind.

Things began for Babis when he first applied to join the police force. His attitude and aptitude had been spotted by the assessors and they had thought that he would be suitable for a large investigation they were commencing.

He was ideal because he spoke both Greek and English fluently, and knew the area of Greece they were particularly interested in. The special police service had approached him soon after his initial training and assessment. They had set out how they could use his skills and talents in a special project, but made it clear to him that it would require a complete personality change and extensive travel between various islands and the UK.

Babis had been very interested to know where this was leading, and what his involvement would be. The commander in chief of the department came to see him and they were locked in serious conversation for almost a day. They had to come up with a plan, a valid reason to explain why Babis would want to leave his home, where in reality, he had been so happy.

He very much loved his parents, and was loved by them. Babis had told the police of his adoption by Mia and Sophia, and how he'd been left by his birth mother. He'd never known anything about his birth mother and never truly wanted to find her.

It came as a big surprise to Babis that the police knew who his birth mother was, along with where she was now living. However, the next bit of information he was to receive had shocked him to the core. He discovered that his birth mother was a drug addict and a dealer known to the police for her activities, and this was why they needed Babis to help.

She was part of a larger drug smuggling and dealing cartel which stretched throughout the entirety of Europe, including the United Kingdom. Although a small cog in a large organisation, this was a way to infiltrate it and eventually make contact with those higher up in the firm. It was a very involved police project, and it was unusual for someone completely new to the force to be asked to undertake this important role.

Babis would have to be seen to leave home while he underwent strict training, and then contact would be made by a special agent acting as his birth mother. The plan initially was for him to return from the police training and act very disappointed upon being rejected. He was to become a seriously dejected individual, unhappy with his lot in life, and then generally begin to mix with a bad crowd.

Once the charade had begun, it genuinely broke his heart to see how hurt his parents were by his attitude and shocking behaviour. It was difficult for him to deal with this, and he spent many hours at first regretting his decision to join the police. Once the sham of his birth mother coming to reclaim him was acted out and he'd convinced his adoptive parents that it was the right thing for him to spend time with her, he was able to move away. It was then easier not to see the sorrow in Mia and Sophia's faces. He longed for his happy carefree life to return, and descended into becoming a rough sleeping, dirty, unkempt individual, so adding to the deception.

He befriended some youths on the island of Kos who were known to the police for their drug involvement. It didn't take long for him to be accepted into the gang, and although it was difficult for him, he began to live rough, sleeping on beaches, begging on street corners and in the squares. He would beg food from tavernas and takeaways. He didn't wash himself or his clothes, and the stench of his own body odour filled his nostrils repulsively! He let his hair grow long and wild and grew a full beard, which he never trimmed. When he caught sight of himself in shop windows, he couldn't believe the man standing there was actually him!

Whilst he was trying to infiltrate the local drug scene, he was shocked to actually be introduced to his real birth mother and discovered to his horror that he had a half-brother who had been groomed by her to become a drug runner, and eventually a dealer.

He was devastated to find that the young boy was also a drug addict who was supplied with drugs as a payment for the role he played in collecting and distributing drugs amongst the addicts on the islands.

Although Babis had some feelings for his birth mother, he was disgusted by the fact that she had used and abused her own son and wondered if that was what his fate would have been, had he not been adopted as a baby by Mia and Sophia, his lovely and caring adoptive mothers.

By day he roamed the streets, at night he slept rough with his mother and half-brother in a derelict stone house on the side of a hill. He hated this existence, but was motivated by the thought of getting his half-brother away from this life of addiction and abuse.

Detailed plans had been made for the ongoing police investigation, but suddenly everything had to be rethought because of the death of Babis' birth mother from an overdose.

He had to become known as a person of interest to the police, and be recognised by the drug gang as a dealer himself.

He was allowed to go to the funeral of his birth mother, but handcuffed and with no other contact. He was surprised to see Sophia and Mia at the cemetery, but had not been allowed to speak, or even acknowledge them. He could see how hurt they were, but now he had to disappear so that he could be taken to another area to once again infiltrate the gang. He tried not to leave a trail, but had underestimated how hard his parents would try to find him. For the police to succeed, he had to completely leave the Greek side of the investigation and become a higher player within the drug dealing cartel.

So much went on behind the scenes, constantly playing the role he'd been given, making new scenarios and continually feeding back information to the investigating team. For Babis, this was scary, as he was always aware that his cover could be blown at any second.

When he left the island of Kos, his descent into relative squalor continued when he slept in shop doorways or under bridges. He collected cardboard boxes from bins and used them to make makeshift shelters, but they didn't last long. When it rained, they became soggy and disintegrated and his few belongings became soiled and wet. He always carried a small plastic bag of cocaine along with a couple of empty bags and a couple of spliffs, so that if challenged, he had the correct props to fit his role. He was moved to yet another island and then to a different country, with little respite from the squalor.

Eventually, Babis was taken to Manchester. He befriended some local addicts who told him where he could get food and sometimes a bed for the night. He went to the Salvation Army centre, where he was given fresh clothes and a winter coat. They encouraged him to take a refreshing shower, with the promise of a hot meal to follow.

He met with other undercover agents to pass on any knowledge he'd gained. For one meeting, he was called to a secret rendezvous in order to meet someone who was to join him out on the streets of Manchester. Part of the plan was for Babis to have a girlfriend who also portrayed the part of a drug user, who he supplied with drugs.

This role was given to another police officer, a girl named Poppy. She was an expert in electronics who could create and install listening devices at the various locations she visited with Babis.

Although their relationship was scripted for them, their feelings for each other eventually grew over the time they spent together.

CHAPTER 6
POPPY

Poppy had been an only child, and was brought up in the outskirts of Manchester. She'd done well at school and went on to university to study forensic science and electronics. She graduated with honours and was now waiting in the foyer to meet her parents at the graduation ceremony. She was so excited at the prospect of making her parents proud of her.

As she stood there the crowds entering became less and less, as families and guests of the graduates took their seats in the main auditorium. Her parents were late and Poppy became anxious, as she would have to join her classmates for the procession to their seats, but there was no sign of them and so reluctantly, she left the foyer. Maybe there had been some traffic problem on their way here, because she knew how much they were looking forward to being there for their daughter.

The ceremony began and Poppy kept searching the audience for any signs of her parents, but couldn't find them amongst the throng of spectators.

Now came the time for her to collect her certificate and as she climbed the stairs to the stage, she took one last look at the audience. All the excitement had now gone and she began to think her parents hadn't made it to her special presentation.

She continued across the stage, shook hands with the Dean of the faculty and accepted her certificate. As she returned to her seat, still searching the crowd of people in the audience, she felt a tap on her shoulder. It was one of her professors gesturing for her to follow him and he led her backstage and motioned to her to go into one of the dressing rooms. Poppy instantly knew something was wrong, but she didn't know how badly wrong things were about to become.

Waiting inside the room were two smartly dressed men and a policewoman in uniform. They asked her to sit down while they slowly gave her the terrible news that her parents had been the victims of a hit and run accident whilst crossing the road. This was shocking enough for Poppy to hear, but what came next took her breath away. She almost fainted at the news!

Both her parents had been rushed to hospital, but unfortunately both were severely injured and did not survive. What should have been a happy family celebration easily became the worst thing she ever had to deal with.

After the ordeal of the joint funeral and the resultant sorting of their effects, Poppy was wondering about the accident. She decided to find out the truth and made an appointment to meet the Chief Constable in Manchester, close to where the accident had taken place. The Chief Constable explained that the driver and passenger in the car were well known drug addicts who were both high on a cocktail of drugs.

They had stolen the car that tragically hit both her parents as they walked across a pelican crossing, which was on red stoplight for vehicles but 'green for go' for pedestrians to cross. It would be some time before the case would come to court, as there were other issues regarding the occupants of the car.

Poppy thanked him for taking the time to explain fully what had happened. She was about to leave the station when Chief Constable Jennings had a question for her.

"Do you have time to listen to a proposal I have for you?" he questioned.

"Of course," she replied curiously. "How can I help you?"

"When I spoke to your university tutors they told me you were the brightest and most accomplished student in the entire year, and anybody who employed you would be lucky to get such a dedicated and hardworking individual. So here I am, hoping to be that lucky employer.

I would like to ask you to join our investigation team as an undercover agent of sorts, working in the drug scene."

As Jennings paused for breath, Poppy couldn't believe what he was saying. Because of the accident and funeral, she'd thought very little about her future and what lay ahead of her. She certainly wanted to work in forensics or electronics, and this could be a way into that area of work.

"You don't have to make a decision right away," Jennings continued. "Come and spend some time with my colleagues and me. We will explain exactly what we do here, and if you feel it's right for you, then I would be delighted to have you with us."

It was a lot for her to take in, but she could feel a sense of excitement about it all.

"What would I have to do?" she asked eventually.

"If you feel up to it, you can start here next Monday. We will get to know each other and set out plans to secure your future with us," Jennings informed the girl, whilst smiling. They chatted a little longer, then shook hands and said their goodbyes.

Poppy mulled it over in her mind as she drove home. It seemed like an excellent proposition. Her immediate thoughts were to talk it through with her parents, but then remembered she was going home to an empty house. She would have to make the decision herself without their guidance.

"Well," she said out loud. "Nothing ventured, nothing gained. Come on, girl, let's give it a go."

Poppy had worked with the Manchester police for several months by now, enjoying the fast pace she'd become accustomed to. Today was the day when she had her review with the boss, and she would receive feedback on the role she'd been taking in the team.

She felt a little nervous as she sat in the office waiting for her boss to enter. The door opened and she turned to see not only her immediate boss, but also Chief Constable Jennings, the man who had recruited her. He came into the room alongside the regional operations manager plus another man, whom she did not recognise. After the shaking of hands, the four sat down and the unknown man began to speak.

"Hello Poppy. I have heard such a lot about you, all of it good, in fact exceptional," the man began.

"Thank you, Sir," Poppy smiled nervously as the man continued.

"Chief Constable Jennings has said that as you are such an asset to the force, he's asked me to run something past you," he stopped, pricking Poppy's interest.

"This is purely voluntary, but we are looking for a female member of staff to go undercover and live a rough life amongst the drug addicts and dealers, both nationally and eventually internationally. It is a very hard role and not without danger, but given your performance so far, we feel it's a role that you could take on." Poppy was intrigued but sat silently while she was told more about the role.

"You would work with another undercover operative and play the part of his girlfriend. The two of you would infiltrate the drug circles and hopefully, eventually the drug cartels." Chief Constable Jennings cocked his head and again smiled at Poppy. "Well, what are your thoughts?" he queried. Poppy smiled but was silent, not sure what to think at this moment in time.

"Okay, we will give you more time to think about it," Jennings suggested. "We will meet again next week, and should you wish to undertake this role, we will bring you up to date with the present situation and outline your training programme."

Poppy went home that day in a haze. Was she dreaming? This was almost the job she had been fantasising about, and it was being offered to her. She would be in for a sleepless night, tossing and turning whilst thinking about it.

A few days later, Poppy, having mulled everything over, made a decision. She was alone now so could do whatever she wished, without upsetting her parents or friends. It would seem it was the job of her dreams and to turn it down might be the biggest mistake of her life.

In the morning, taking the bull by the horns she marched into the office and informed the team she would be thrilled to take on the role spoken about.

Her training began immediately. It would be long and hard, but soon things would change for her.

For Poppy, today was the day when her life would change forever. Today would become completely different to anything she'd ever known before.

She was usually so smartly turned out and her hair was always nicely styled and shiny. Her nails were manicured and her makeup perfect, but now – Wow! - What a transformation! She hardly recognised herself as she looked at the reflection in the mirror.

Her hair had been bleached and had dark roots from the re-growth, and was dirty! It looked like it hadn't been washed for ages. Her nails appeared bitten and dirty. Her clothes were scruffy and she wore a food stained t-shirt, ripped jeans and filthy battered trainers. She also had a tatty bag hung from her shoulder.

'Oh, my god,' she thought. 'I look like someone off the streets,' which of course, was just how they wanted her appearance to be.

She began to wonder what her co-worker would be like. She'd been told he'd already been working undercover for a while. Her role was to be seen as his girlfriend, who would also become known as a regular drug user.

She heard a knock on the door. "Come in," she whispered nervously. The door opened and her intake of breath was audible.

"I know," the man said. "I look, and smell, horrendous!" He held his hand out to her. "Hi, I'm Babis," he said. "I believe we are to become a couple, that is if you can stand being anywhere near me," he smiled. Poppy hesitated for a moment, but then offered her hand for him to shake.

"I'm Poppy," she said, "and I'm pleased to meet you, I think."

They both smiled when meeting each other, realising that they would have to get much better acquainted if they were to become a couple in the eyes of the dealers. What was nice though was that they both felt at ease with each other, even though their appearance was somewhat scruffy and extremely dirty.

They were to spend the next few days together, whilst they were briefed on their roles and given the latest up to date information about the operation as it progressed.

They both knew that they played a small part in a massive operation regarding drug cartels, drug lords, and all the horrors that trade in illegal drugs brought to society. They were players in a much bigger plan, stretching across many countries.

They got to know details on a need to know only basis, and as such, were small pawns in a much bigger game. However, their roles were important and vital to the operation.

Babis was to return to the streets and to the life he thoroughly detested, but he knew it wouldn't be forever. When Poppy finally joined him he introduced her to Sam, the man who Babis insisted went with him after the death of his mother.

He had up to date knowledge of the drug hierarchy, and as such was a great asset.

During the nights when Babis and Poppy cuddled up together to keep warm, Sam would always stay close by. They walked the streets together, never letting Sam know they were acting, simply acting. They shared food and even blankets during the colder nights. One or both of them, would make up an excuse to be alone when they went to report back, or Poppy had to place bugs or cameras in certain places.

They quickly became a good team, even though Sam was not aware of it. His knowledge of the places and availability of drugs helped them tremendously. Hopefully the culmination of all their hard work and deception would soon arrive.

Unbeknown to them, much work had been going on behind the scenes in Manchester, where special operations had been monitoring events via devices planted in neighbouring flats and buildings.

The events of this night would change Babis' life forever. He and Poppy were to meet with a person much higher up the ladder within the drug gang, a man who was looking to recruit them for a more involved job than the one they'd been acting out. They had been told to go to a flat in the Moss Side area of Manchester. This information had been passed to the police.

Both Poppy and Babis knew this was a highly dangerous situation to place each other in, but they had every confidence in their colleagues, who they knew would be close by at all times.

They stood on the street corner with their shoulders hunched. Babis put his arm around Poppy's shoulders and whispered in her ear. "We've got this, girl," he told her.

His phone rang and he got a brief message telling him to go to the block of flats situated immediately opposite where they currently were, where somebody would be waiting for them.

"Here we go," Babis said, with a hint of nerves in his voice.

Poppy took hold of his hand and smiled in his direction. "Don't worry, Babis. I know you will look after me," she reassured him. "Come on, let's go," she commanded.

A man met them at the bottom of a flight of stairs that led to a first-floor apartment. He gestured to them to climb the stairs and then followed closely behind them, all the time glancing round to check if they were being watched or followed.

If they let down their guard now, everything could have been in vain. All the nights spent in cold dank, dirty and squalid doorways for months on end, with only each other for warmth and comfort, would have all been for nothing.

The man who'd met them stepped in front of them to knock on the paint blistered door. Babis and Poppy each held their breath, as they heard the click of a lock being turned. They were ushered into a smoke-filled room where two men were seated on a battered settee. They stood in front of them whilst they were searched to see if they were carrying anything they shouldn't have in their pockets. The men found a couple of small re-sealable bags, which had previously held cocaine and still contained two half smoked spliffs.

One of the seated men nodded to the man who'd brought Babis and Poppy into the room and he left the apartment, along with the two of them. Poppy and Babis felt uneasy, but this was what they'd been working towards for such a long time.

Questions were asked of them to test their commitment and knowledge of the drug dealing operations they had been involved in. A proposal was then made regarding them joining the team.

"What's in it for us?" Babis asked, with a cocky tone and a smile on his face, not wanting to sound too eager.

"That depends on how good you are at the job, and whether you can be relied on," one of the men, whom Babis thought was in charge of the other, said.

Further details were revealed. Babis didn't want to push too much, but he knew that the operation teams were listening in on the conversation, so he needed to ask a few more mundane questions.

"Okay, we will be in touch. You can go now," the second of the men said, motioning them towards the door.

"You know we will be watching you from now on," the first man told them sinisterly as Poppy and Babis turned to leave. When hearing this, Poppy felt a shiver run down her spine.

They opened the door and staggered down the stairs, glad to be out of the room. However, as they reached the entrance onto the parking lot in front of the flats, all hell broke out.

They could hear their colleagues breaking into the apartment, and the phrase, "Armed police. Stay where you are," being shouted.

Babis and Poppy continued to walk away from the building. As they did so, they heard shots being fired from within the apartment block. Suddenly there was gunfire from another block across from the car park, and the gunfire was coming in their direction.

As Babis turned to face where the gunfire was coming from, to his horror he saw that Poppy had been hit. She went down injured, but the gunfire continued.

Without a thought for his safety, Babis threw himself on top of Poppy and lay there feigning his own death. Eventually the gunfire ceased and Babis picked up the limp body of his partner and carried her to safety behind a parked car. He cautiously raised his head and frantically called out to anyone who could hear. "Officer down, get an ambulance – NOW!"

He held Poppy tightly, holding her close to him as he spoke softly in her ear. "Don't leave me. I won't let you go. You can't die. I need you. I love you."

After what seemed like an eternity, two ambulance men ran across the car park to where Poppy lay, after first being given the all clear by the supervising officer on the scene. They carried Poppy to the waiting ambulance, lifting her gently onboard. Babis tried to climb in to be with her.

"I'm sorry, Sir, but we cannot allow you to travel with us if you are not related," the ambulance driver ordered.

Babis uttered the first words that came into his head. "But she's my partner," he whimpered. The crew relented and allowed him inside to travel with Poppy. Babis thanked God that the word, 'partner,' was now seen as synonymous with the word, 'wife.'

The ambulance men set up a drip and attempted to stem the flow of blood from the gunshot wound. Babis held tightly to Poppy's hand as they blue lighted her across Manchester to a nearby hospital.

When they arrived outside the building, some of the staff were there already there waiting with a gurney, ready to rush Poppy into the 'Accident and Emergency' department. Although reluctant to do so, Babis let go of Poppy's hand and relinquished her care to the professionals.

He followed as far as he was allowed, but was then asked to wait in the corridor whilst the 'A and E' department did what they could to save her life

In all his years alive on this earth, Babis had never felt this alone. All he could do now was to wait patiently for news of the woman who he now realised was the love of his life. The thought of losing her was unthinkable. He had grown to love her grubby appearance, her unkempt hair, and her crooked little smile.

He put his head in his hands and cried openly. The guilt he felt at not protecting her was intolerable. Poppy had told him she knew he would look after her, but he hadn't.

After what seemed like an eternity, a nurse came to tell Babis. "We have moved Poppy into her own private room," she said softly to the waiting Babis.

"Can I see her?" he questioned.

"You can sit with her but she will be unresponsive, as we have sedated her. She is still drowsy, and will be for a couple of hours yet," the nurse replied.

"Thank you nurse," Babis said, almost in a whisper. He then went to be at Poppy's side.

He sat by her bedside, hardly taking his eyes off her. There were machines monitoring any fluctuations in her heartbeat or breathing. She was attached to drips which were replacing the blood she'd lost. Her face appeared as white as the sheets which covered her.

He remembered what a family member had told him about when her husband had been involved in a horrendous accident, and how his life had been in the balance. He had sustained horrific injuries, so bad that he had had to have part of his leg amputated. She'd told how she had continuously spoken to him although he was unconscious, as the staff had told her that hearing was the sense that remained the longest. She said how she'd prayed for him to survive.

He wasn't a religious man but Babis prayed for the life of Poppy, his partner, only leaving her side when the nurses came in to tend to her bandages, or move her to prevent bedsores. He would watch the physiotherapist manipulating her legs and arms to prevent muscle wastage. Sometimes he'd walk around the hospital grounds deep in thought, thinking about why he hadn't been able to protect her, and how had it all gone so wrong.

He'd been told that the sting had been successful and they had played a pivotal part in bringing many criminals to justice, but Babis could only think what an expensive price to pay. What a waste of a precious life, if Poppy didn't make it.

Day after day there was no change in Poppy as the doctors continued to keep her in the induced coma while her body was given time to heal from the trauma. On some days he felt strong and would talk to Poppy for hours, telling her what he planned for their futures together, while at other times he just held her hand, feeling utter despair for what he might be faced with.

He felt immense guilt for having failed to keep her safe and it ate into him. When he did sleep, he was plagued with nightmares going over and over again at what had happened.

Babis couldn't tell his mothers about the horrors he'd witnessed, or the days and nights he had prayed to God to keep him alive. He couldn't relate how he and Poppy had been caught up in a gun battle on the streets, and how Poppy had been hit by a bullet and Babis had carried her limp body from the scene, risking his own life to rescue her.

He had sat at the hospital now for a number of days and nights, just watching her while machines kept her alive. The immense joy he'd experienced when she was finally taken off the ventilator and opened her eyes to see him sat by her bedside, was incredible.

She'd managed half a smile before her eyes closed again, but Babis knew she was a fighter and this was the first step on her road to recovery. Seeing this made him realise just how much she meant to him. She'd been his partner at work for some time, and now she was his partner in his heart. He now knew he also wanted her to be his partner in life.

There was so much he wanted to tell his mothers and it seemed unfair that he couldn't yet tell them about Sam, the half-brother he had come to love. He'd been silent for a while and Mia and Sophia could tell it was heart wrenching what he was reliving.

"I really can't tell you anything," he told them apologetically.

"You will in time," Mia said as reassuringly as possible.

"Maybe I will never be able to tell you, ever," Babis added.

Mia and Sophia wondered what could have happened, but accepted that, perhaps when he was ready, he would tell them something.

"Now please listen to what I want you to do. I will have to stay here in Manchester for a while, but I promise you I will be coming back to Kos soon," Babis told the two of them, bringing a little bit of hope into their lives. He then continued, "I will be working as a police officer at Antimachia police station, so I will be once again living in Kefalos, where I belong."

"That's great news, son," Mia gushed.

"There is a lot still to be sorted here," Babis continued, "so I have to stay on until everything is completed, but I promise I will ring you every day. I also promise I will never leave you again."

The two mums were delighted with what Babis had just told them, although they really would have liked him to return to Kefalos with them today.

"I really have to go now," he told them, holding his arms out for a hug. It was hard for Mia and Sophia to see him walk through the door and leaving them alone in the room.

A few seconds later, the man who'd brought them there came in and told them he would take them back to their hotel.

When they arrived, he got out of the car and shook hands with Mia and Sophia.

"You may not understand at present, but your son has been magnificent," he announced. "You should be really proud of him. I can see just how much he means to you. I want to thank you for sharing your son with us."

"It's our pleasure," the two women smiled, now very relieved that Babis was back in their lives again.

Have a safe flight, ladies," he said. With this, he returned to the car and drove away.

Still feeling shocked by what had happened, and going over and over in their minds what had been said, they tried to make some sense of it all. However, in truth they couldn't, and only time would tell.

When they returned to Kos, and Kefalos in particular, there were great celebrations with all the family when they were able to say that they had at last found Babis. They were able to tell the family that he was well, if a little underweight for such a big guy. The family asked so many questions, although they were not able to give answers.

Mia finally stood and held up her hands to stop all the shouting and questions.

"I'm sorry," she said. "I know you want to know everything, but we know as little as you do. Let us just be happy that Babis is coming back to us, and he is alive and well."

Glasses were raised, and from the religious amongst them, thanks were given to God for the safe return of Babis. Now they all waited in anticipation for his safe return to the island.

CHAPTER 7
SAM

Sam had been kept in a safe house whilst the operation was brought to a conclusion, but was suffering badly because of his addiction.

Babis hadn't yet told Mia and Sophia about his half-brother, or about Poppy, but he knew if things went well and Sam was successful in dealing with his addiction, he would definitely want him to be part of his life.

He knew the journey for Sam would be a torturous one, and knew there would be times when he would want to go back to the drugs that had given him release in the past.

Babis had an appointment at the rehab centre in Manchester, which was run by a charitable organisation with many successful results. The cost of the treatment at the centre would be met by the police federation as a thank you for the help Sam had given them whilst on the streets with Babis and Poppy.

Babis had been sent some literature from the rehab centre which he'd read, but he still needed questions answered. The literature spoke of a twelve-step approach to addiction. Although it was originally a religious based recovery, the steps had been adapted to have a non-religious emphasis whilst maintaining a spiritual one –

Step 1 - Addicts admit that addiction has taken over their life to the extent that they cannot control it. They also acknowledge that addiction destroys an addict's life, and the life of their loved ones.

Step 2 - Patients accept that some higher power can help them overcome addiction, if they also try themselves.

Step 3 – Addicts make a decision to accept the higher power, as they recognise them as the one who can turn their lives around, submitting themselves to his will.

Step 4 - The recovering addicts search their souls and identify all the wrongs they caused for themselves and others.

Step 5 - After soul searching, addicts are encouraged to admit the wrongs they have been doing. The admission is not only to themselves, but to the higher being and other human beings. It helps put aside their ego and provides an opportunity for growth.

Step 6 – Addicts become ready to accept the higher being's guidance in removing these shortcomings. This phase prepares members to submit themselves to the higher power believing that it can help them remove all the shortfalls of their personalities, actions and behaviours.

Step 7 - Addicts ask the power to remove their shortcomings by acknowledging their powerlessness. It teaches humility, and they become better human beings.

Step 8 - Patients in recovery make a list of people they might have hurt by their addictive or harmful behaviour and take actions to make amends to them. They are encouraged to think about all the people they might have harmed during addiction, and be one hundred percent willing to make amends with them and ask for forgiveness.

Step 9 - They make sincere efforts to amend relations with those they have wronged and members are encouraged to make amends with everyone. This phase calls for the practical application of the previous phase where they are encouraged to make amends to everyone. Once amends are made and forgiveness sought, it serves as excellent medicine for the soul.

Step 10 - Members are urged to continue searching their souls and making amends as soon as they realise them. It shows them the importance of this aspect as being a continuous process instead of a one-off process.

Step 11 - During this step members accept the idea of a bigger plan that the higher power has for everyone. It helps them maintain spiritual progress, while aiming to become better and clean from drugs.

Step 12 - The last stage guides members to be of service to other members of society to help them overcome addiction and practice all these phases in all walks of their life after recovery.

Babis was a little unsure whether the programme would suit Sam, although he knew something had to be done immediately to get him away from a life of drugs. He was introduced to the manageress and had many questions to ask about the programme, wanting to support his half-brother in any way he could.

"My name is Rebecca," the manageress smiled, as she shook hands with, and introduced herself to Babis.

She began by saying how she would outline how the programme worked, but first she needed to ask Babis a few questions about Sam and his relationship to him.

Babis explained to Rebecca about his own adoption, about meeting his birth mother and then discovering he had a half-brother, Sam. It was difficult not to tell the whole story, but he was unable to do so.

He told Rebecca that Sam's mother had used and abused him when he was young, and had led him to a life of drug use and drug dealing. His mother had died and now Babis was his only blood relative.

He wanted Sam to have a better life than that controlled by drugs, and had spoken to him about the possibility of getting him on to a residential rehab programme.

"Thank you for sharing this with me, it can't have been easy for you," Rebecca said, after listening to the story. "Knowing the background of a potential resident helps us to determine the initial steps we have to take."

Rebecca explained to Babis how the programme was created, and how the centre focused greatly on peer groups and in attending various meetings like Narcotics Anonymous, along with Alcoholics Anonymous.

They would use the template of the twelve-step programme, initiated originally by Alcoholics Anonymous. This was the programme which Babis had previously read about.

Rebecca told him that they used powerful peer pressure in support groups that help people recover from substance use disorders, behavioural addictions, and sometimes mental health conditions. It also helps people achieve, and maintain, abstinence from substances.

There would be a group meeting with fellow residents each day, and also one-to-one mentoring from residents who were further along in the programme.

Sam would be accompanied at all times by senior members if he were ever to leave the centre for whatever reason. A key worker would be appointed for Sam, who would spend time with him to coach and help him. There would always be someone there to support Sam through what would be a difficult time.

The programme would lead him through emotional and physically tortuous times, as he learnt to live his life without drugs controlling his body and mind.

Sam would be interviewed to see if he was ready and willing to undertake the rehab, and to see if he was fully committed to it. This was all down to Sam himself, and nobody else.

Babis was hoping and praying that Sam would want to take part in this. He thanked Rebecca for seeing him and explaining everything to him. He hoped Sam would be able to cope, but he could tell there was a great amount of support for him, here at the centre. Now, the time had come to arrange an interview for his half-brother.

Sam was desperate to succeed, as his life thus far had been a miserable one. He'd been used and abused by his own mother, and had never known who his father was.

A strange feeling now stirred within him, a feeling that he'd never felt before. He now had a brother who cared about him, a brother who truly wanted to include him in his life and wanted him to succeed. Sam felt a pang of emotion, maybe also for the first time in his life.

He'd never really felt or been loved, or truly loved anyone, including himself. Drugs had been his constant companion, momentary relief from the disgusting life he was living. This was a once in a lifetime chance to rid himself of the squalor and to gain some self-esteem, to be accepted by others, not for what he was selling to them, but because he was liked for who he really was.

A lump formed in his throat, whilst he felt dampness in his eyes. He couldn't remember the last time he'd cried. It must have been as a small child when his mother abandoned him in his cot, whilst she left the house to find the drugs she couldn't live without! He learned then that crying didn't bring anyone to him.

He remembered how his wet nappy had hung, stinking to his ulcerated body. The sheets in his cot were stiff and the mattress was full of flies and bugs. His stomach would rumble, as he'd not eaten adequate food for days on end. His mom drifted in and out of their home, but he was kept well out of the way whilst she earned a little money selling her body to anyone desperate enough to use her.

As he grew older he was a quiet and withdrawn child, but soon he would become a runner, taking his life into his own hands and crossing busy streets to deliver packages to people waiting on street corners, and then returning home with money for his mother. In return for this, as he grew a little older his mother would give him pills that made him forget the miserable life he led.

These pills took him briefly to somewhere where he felt safe and secure, but the feeling was short lived and the need for the sensation of release became more and more intense. The addiction to drugs ruled his life from then on. He just wanted to feed his habit and had little interest in anything else.

The thought of quitting his addiction to drugs really scared Sam. He knew how bad he felt when he needed drugs and couldn't obtain them. Now he would have to deal with that over and over again, during his recovery. When times had been hard, drugs had always helped him through it.

He had been told that at the centre, he would have a room of his own. There would be clean sheets on his bed and a place to keep his belongings. He would be given three good meals a day to help him put on some weight, as he was far too underweight for the age they believed him to be. This sounded good to Sam. He would be allowed a small amount of cash each week to buy toiletries or treats, whilst everything else would be provided for him.

He had grown to love Babis and wanted him and Poppy to be proud of him, but wondered if he was strong enough to conquer his addiction. This was the reason he was in here, but did he have the motivation to succeed? Only he could decide this, and he had to make this decision for himself.

The road to recovery would be long and hard with many occasions when he would want to give up, but then he thought again of the other option, alone in the world, no home and no money, living a life of squalor and probably a life of crime, along with ultimately a slow and horrid death!

He knew he didn't want this and so made the decision to enter the rehab programme, where he knew he had plenty of support both inside and outside from Babis and Poppy.

When he arrived at the centre for his induction, he was given a fresh set of clothes, along with lovely smelling clean sheets for his bed. Having his own room felt just like living in a palace, as he'd never had anywhere private before. The arduous journey ahead would now begin for Sam, and he was ready for the struggle!

CHAPTER 8
THE TORTURE BEGINS

Babis had received an urgent phone call as he was the registered next-of-kin for Sam, and so was the first point of contact if anything was amiss. He listened carefully as a member of staff at the rehab unit explained how Sam had been going through a particularly difficult time and had been unable to control his temper, damaging equipment belonging to the centre and smashing up his room.

"I will pay for any damage caused," Babis was quick to say. However, he was told that Sam had to admit to the wrong he'd done and to understand why he did it, before they would look at how he could redress what he had done.

The manageress of the centre felt that Sam needed a visit from someone close to him. Babis was the only family he had, so he agreed he would get there as soon as possible.

As yet, Babis hadn't told Mia and Sophia about Sam. He had decided to wait and see how his half-brother progressed with his rehab, before introducing him to the family. A little white lie to the two women was all that was needed, saying he had to go to a meeting in Manchester at short notice. Mia and Sophia did not question him, as his work had been his secret from them for a long time.

Babis travelled to the airport the next morning, having secured a seat on a holiday flight from Kos to Manchester. It seemed strange that whilst in the airport, he was surrounded by sad holiday makers on their way home after their time enjoying Kos. Some of them suffered with very red faces, caused by too many hours in the Greek sunshine.

He booked a seat with extra leg room at the front of the plane, and was surprised when no one occupied the other two seats. He positioned himself by the window, as the plane ambled down the track leading to the runway. It slowed to a stop, pausing only for a few seconds before the pilot revved up the engines to full throttle, released the brakes, and catapulted the plane along the runway at breakneck speed and eventually into flight.

It was a beautifully clear day today and as they took off, the magnificent blue Aegean Sea was dotted with small craft. They passed over very small islands as they continued to climb up to what would eventually be their cruising height and airspeed.

Babis knew that a car would be waiting at the airport to transport him onwards and he began to relax a little. Not realising how tired he was he soon began to feel drowsy, and quickly fell into a deep and fitful slumber. He was still plagued by nightmares regarding the terrible night when they were caught up in a gunfight with drug gangs.

"Poppy – Poppy," Babis was shouting. The air hostess came and asked if he was okay.

"Can I get you anything?" she enquired.

At that moment, Babis realised he'd woken from his slumber and was calling Poppy's name. He felt really embarrassed.

"It was just a bad dream," he informed the pretty hostess. "I'm sorry if I disturbed anyone."

"Not at all," she assured him. "Not wishing to pry," she questioned, "but is Poppy your wife?"

Babis smiled. "Not yet, but I hope she will be one day," he replied.

"Would you like anything to eat or drink?" she asked. "You were fast asleep when the trolley came round?"

"Could I have a strong coffee please, with lots of sugar? It will help me to focus on what I have to deal with," he requested, and then went back to looking out through his window.

It didn't seem too long before they were beginning the descent into Manchester. When they arrived, Babis passed quickly through passport control, and having only hand luggage he went straight through to the arrivals lounge.

He scoured the cards being held up by taxi drivers but didn't see his name displayed, but then an arm was raised in the crowd and he heard his name being called.

His heart skipped a beat, for standing there waiting for him was Poppy. He could not believe it. He opened his arms wide and she leapt into them. They hugged each other tightly, so happy to see each other – what a welcome.

Arm in arm they walked to the car park. Poppy's little MX5 car was quite small for Babis, even though he had no luggage to carry. All the time they kept glancing at each other, as if not really believing they were together again. Neither spoke for some time until Babis finally broke the silence.

"How did you know I was coming?" he questioned.

"The centre phoned me. I know that I didn't tell you, but I have been liaising with the rehab staff about Sam, and I have gone in to chat with him a few times. I know it was difficult for you to get here, so I took your place on visiting days." Hearing this made Babis feel very happy. He smiled as Poppy continued.

"I've grown very fond of Sam and have learned so much about drug addiction. He's told me about the things he's been doing, and how he's been learning about the fact that it's a disease as much as it's an addiction. He had been led into it by his mother, and drugs have been his only escape from the sordid lifestyle he was living."

Babis felt very emotional. This was the woman he had grown to love, and he hoped one day she would agree to marry him. Now here she was accepting his half-brother in just the same way as him.

"Thank you so much for spending time with Sam. It means so much to me," Babis gushed.

"You're welcome," Poppy replied.

"Even though I love my two mothers, Sam is the only true blood relative I have, so he is special to me," Babis continued. "I was hoping so much that the treatment here at the rehab centre would be successful, and that he would have a much better life than he had previously."

"I know how much you care for him, just as I do now," Poppy told him. "I have got to know him outside of the drug scenario we were involved in."

"I haven't told my mums' about that, because they've had enough to deal with these past few years, and I don't want them to be hurt so cruelly again," Babis reasoned.

"I understand that," Poppy agreed, "but they love you so much and are proud of what you have achieved. Sam is a part of you, so I'm sure they will be prepared to help and they will accept him. Let's go and see what's been happening with him."

They drove to the rehab centre and the manageress was there to greet them. She took them into her office. No introductions were necessary as Poppy had been a regular visitor there. Babis was feeling very anxious about the situation.

"Firstly, I must tell you that we've been impressed by Sam's commitment to the programme," Mrs. Rodham, the manageress told them. "We've been very pleased with Sam's progress, I must say. He has worked hard to complete the steps of the programme. He's spoken openly at meetings about his addiction, encouraging others to do the same. He's been volunteering with local charities helping the homeless and addicts, and he's really shone at that role.

"This all sounds great," Babis offered.

"Very encouraging," Poppy agreed, joining in with the conversation.

"We have had great feedback on how he has spent time, both making meals for them and chatting with them, explaining what help is available," Mrs. Rodham informed the two, as they listened intently. However, then she said, "Unfortunately........."

"Oh no, here it comes," Babis muttered in dismay.

"We had a little blip. Sam has been allowed to go out unaccompanied on several occasions and we have never had any problems with that. However, he returned two days ago and became really agitated. This was so unlike him and we could see that something was wrong," Mrs. Rodham stopped and looked at Babis.

"How so?" he queried.

"When he was asked about it, he became very angry and aggressive towards the staff here. He began damaging furniture and the contents of his room. His key worker finally calmed him down and found out why he was so angry." Seeing she had both Babis and Poppy's attention now, Mrs Rodham continued.

"The aggression was actually aimed at himself. Whilst helping a homeless person at the charity he'd been offered cocaine. Worst still, he accepted it, using it along with the person he was supposedly helping.

The tantrum had been because he was so ashamed at what he'd done. He felt he had let everyone down. He had gained trust but now felt the trust was broken. He was so angry with himself and was unable at first to deal with that anger."

Babis wasn't sure if he felt angry or sad at what he'd just heard, but continued to listen.

"Sam was afraid that he would be thrown off the programme and returned to the sordid, squalid life, which he had before. He begged to come back, wanting to make amends to all those he'd let down," she stopped and looked at the two.

Poppy could hardly control her emotions, whilst Babis felt deep anger as this was a once in a lifetime lifeline chance that

Sam had been given. He felt disappointed in Sam, for the disrespect he had apparently shown for the people who were doing their best to support him.

Rebecca Rodham, the manageress, went on to say that it was not unusual for long term addicts to break the rules, once their freedom was extended. Many never returned and they went back to the addiction. Some returned after a short time having realised they couldn't exist that way anymore, but Sam had come back immediately and told the staff at the centre what he'd done.

"He was unable to control his anger and self-loathing, and had destroyed everything in his room," Rebecca stated. "Once he'd calmed down, they could see the remorse and the shame he felt, along with the disappointment he was experiencing. The members of the team held a meeting, where it was decided he would stay at the centre as long as he was prepared to work part of the programme again. Since then, he's been tested regularly and his results are clean."

Babis didn't know what to say, and Poppy could see how upset he was. She held onto his hand and squeezed it, bringing him back to his senses.

"So, what happens now?" Babis asked.

"As long as he completes the necessary steps and continues to stay clean, he can remain here. When he's ready, he will be allowed levels of freedom whilst he tries out his own resistance to temptation. We do believe he really does want to beat it," Rebecca informed the two. She then went on to explain more to them, which helped Babis to relax.

In turn, Babis asked questions which were quickly and positively answered. He knew there may be more questions which he would have liked answers to, but the meeting had to be terminated, as Rebecca had other duties to perform at the centre.

"Would you like to see Sam now?" Rebecca questioned Babis, but he didn't answer.

"You should go alone," Poppy said, seeing the hesitation his face.

"No Poppy, we will go together," Babis finally replied. "You are as much a part of his life as I am," he told her.

As they entered, Sam was in his room sitting on his bed. A window was still boarded up and they could see the remains of a chair that Sam was trying to repair. Sam didn't look at them, and he seemed embarrassed.

"Sam, it's okay buddy," Babis said, speaking in a reassuringly quiet tone. "We know what's happened."

"I let you down badly," Sam said, with a pained expression upon his face.

"No," Babis said firmly. "Your addiction is what caused the problem, not you. If you really mean it, and want to rid yourself of this illness you must not beat yourself up, but learn to control and master the addiction, as well as your actual behaviour."

"I know, I know," Sam said with his head in his hands.

They sat together for a while not really saying very much, but when it was time for them to leave, Sam stood and offered his hand to Babis.

"Come here," Babis smiled, wrapping his arms around Sam. They hugged for a while and then Poppy stepped forward and hugged him too. All three felt very emotional.

Babis called in to thank Rebecca, the manageress, before he and Poppy returned to the car. Neither spoke for some time, both being deep in thought. He was due to return to Kos that evening, which meant he would soon have to leave for the airport.

He would have loved to have been able to spend more time with Poppy, but was grateful for the little time they'd had.

They grabbed a coffee and were enjoying a little small talk, when suddenly an idea popped into his head.

"Poppy, I would love you to come to Kos," Babis said. "I would love you to come to Kefalos and meet the rest of the family."

"We'll see," was her reply.

It was a quick goodbye at the airport, as parking was costly if you lingered. An hour or so later, Babis felt very alone as he boarded the plane for the flight home.

He was happy to have seen Sam, even if his half-brother was at a low point in his recovery. What Rebecca Rodham had told them had given him fresh hope that Sam would make it through, and hopefully he would make a full recovery.

Later that evening, being back at home made him rethink about what he wanted in his life, he wanted Poppy, and he also wanted Sam.

He also wanted to continue working out of Antimachia police station, and wanted to be able to hold his head high and be accepted again in the village. The fact was that none of the villagers knew what Babis had been doing over the recent years. They still held him responsible for the death of his birth mother, even though it had all been part of the charade.

He knew he would have to prove himself worthy of their acceptance, and that would take time. However, he was prepared to wait and earn their respect.

Babis disguised his regular trips to the rehab centre to see Sam under the pretence of further training for work and help with the upcoming trial of the men he'd helped to arrest. Sam had now completed Stage One of the rehab programme, comprising the twelve steps, and had now graduated to Stage Two.

Many of the staff congratulated him on his progress, as well as his peers on the programme, who praised him for his determination and commitment. Babis had agreed that the latter end of Stage Two could be completed by having a mentor and support mechanisms in place on the island of Kos. Sam was delighted with the promise of moving to the island to be with his big brother.

Now it was up to Babis to tell Mia and Sophia about Sam and ask if they would let him into their lives. His regular visits to England involved him meeting up with Poppy and spending time with her.

Her own recovery was progressing well, and like Babis, she had received specialist counselling after the event that almost claimed her life.

Babis was besotted with Poppy and planned to ask her to marry him just as soon as she was fully fit again, although he wasn't sure how he would do it.

He had mentioned to her before about her taking up an admin role with the police force on Kos, and was happy when she told him that she'd give it some thought.

"Thank you," he'd gushed, when hearing her reply.

Poppy's feelings for Babis had deepened and her eyes lit up when he went to visit her. They had progressed from small hugs to fully embracing, holding tightly onto each other when they met after a month's separation. She wanted to be with Babis and she loved the Greek islands. It all seemed too good to be true. Here was an opportunity to be with the man she'd grown to love, and to be on the idyllic Greek island of Kos.

Whilst her bodily wounds had healed, the mental torment of the events still consumed her at times, and she wondered if this would ever leave her. Her nightmares had lessened over time, with waking up in a cold sweat and feeling terrified, was now less frequent than it had been.

Maybe she was ready for a change; maybe life without this worry was just what she needed. She still wondered if it was feelings of guilt when Babis had been unable to protect her during the shooting incident that was fuelling his feelings for her. She wondered whether he really loved her as much as he appeared to.

Babis actually kept his feelings close to his chest. He didn't want to scare Poppy away. He suggested that she paid a visit to Kos for perhaps a month, whilst she was still technically on sick leave.

Babis and Poppy went together to attend Sam's graduation ceremony, knowing he could move from the rehab centre into a flat provided by the centre, where he would be closely monitored and regularly tested for drugs.

It was a strange transition, likened to a choker chain and short lead having been used for six months, then being replaced by an extended lead, which could give him more freedom, but could be reeled in if anything untoward was to happen.

Now came the time for the big question, the big question for Mia and Sophia. Babis needed to know if they would be prepared to accept his half-brother, Sam, into their lives. He explained to them that, currently in rehab, Sam would need lots of support when he was discharged. He would be technically homeless and with no family except for Babis.

Mia and Sophia had welcomed their much-loved son back home to Kefalos. Each and every day now, he was looking more like the man they feared they'd lost. They all spent quality time together, and Kali was always there with them, if she knew he would be calling.

Life was returning to normal, however, Mia and Sophia would notice that Babis was sometimes a little distant and they wondered what was going on in his head. Was he reliving a bad time, or wishing for something more than the life he now had here, which had never been an issue before he left. They thought that something was definitely missing in his life.

On one visit, Kali was out, so Babis sat Mia and Sophia down and told them he had something very important to ask them. He wanted them to think very carefully about his question before they gave him an answer.

"During my time away, I found I had a half-brother," Babis began. "His name is Sam, and he was badly treated by my birth mother. She used him as a drug runner, and also fed him drugs to the point at which he became severely addicted to them. He is now in rehab, but will soon be allowed come out.

I would like Sam to come here and live in Kefalos. There are plans in place to continue with his recovery here on the island, and there would be lots of help from all the authorities. However, what is needed most is a stable home environment, where he would be loved unconditionally."

Babis stopped to take breath. He scanned his mothers' to judge their reaction before popping the big question.

"Mum," he said to Mia, "Mum," he said to Sophia, "I want to ask you if you think we could let Sam join our family. He has no one, only me." Again he looked into their eyes and searched Mia and Sophia's faces for a reaction. The two women looked at each other. They had a big decision to make.

Many years ago, they had made the decision to adopt Babis, and at the time, Kali had been too young to ask for her approval. Now the two felt it was only right to confer with Kali to ask how she felt about Sam joining the fold. After all, to her he was a stranger.

Once Babis had repeated his story and request to Kali, she was quick to give her answer. "It will be great to have another brother," she beamed.

Kali had missed Babis so much whilst he had been away, and was really looking forward to spending lots of time with him now.

There would be a great deal to arrange, but they could still remember the joy and excitement from when they first brought Babis home, along with the thrill of actually adopting him.

He had caused them a lot of heartache lately, but they were all so proud of what he had done. He was asking them from his heart to accept his half-brother, and they couldn't do anything other than accept and agree to help.

A room was prepared for Sam. A mentor was arranged for him at the centre, where he would continue with the recovery programme. Now it was a waiting game until Babis could bring Sam out to meet them all. He was about to tell them about another person who was due to arrive with Sam, but he decided to surprise his mothers instead.

This was the day they had all been waiting for. The plane taxied down the runway at Kos airport and came to a halt outside Arrivals. Steps were taken to the entrance door and passengers disembarked, crossing the tarmac to the bus that would take them on the very short transfer to the door of the Arrivals lounge.

They spotted Babis with his arm around the shoulders of Sam. He looked quite small next to Babis, and had changed from the skinny unkempt young boy whom Babis had first met, and was now a healthy looking teenager.

Sophia and Mia were trying to keep their emotions in check, but couldn't resist running forward to embrace their son, and now their potential second son.

Babis kept glancing back towards the Arrivals lounge and baggage reclaim. Sophia and Mia wondered if he had forgotten something. He released himself from his mothers' embrace and walked back towards the door of Arrivals. A slim figure of a woman emerged through the gate. Babis ran excitedly towards her, took hold and lifted her into the air. He was beaming with delight and then kissed the young woman.

Sophia and Mia were baffled. Babis had told them about a special female colleague he'd worked with, but she lived in England. Little did they know that each time Babis went to visit Sam in the rehab centre, he had also spent time with Poppy. Their relationship had deepened and finally Poppy had agreed to come to Kos and meet his mothers. Of course, being his mothers' meant that they both recognised just how smitten their son was with this beautiful young woman.

Introductions were made, but the promise was also made to tell the full story about how they'd become close, and how they now couldn't imagine not being together.

Following the twenty minute drive from the airport, they would introduce Sam to his new home. Although he appeared a little shy, he would soon relax and come to realise that his life would be so much better now than his previous one. There were people here who would accept him into the family and give him the love and support he'd so missed out on in his life.

After a few days of settling in, a family gathering was arranged where Sam and Poppy would meet and get to know all the other relatives from within this loving, extended family.

CHAPTER 9
LIFE IN KEFALOS

Poppy had been in Kefalos now for about six weeks and had fallen in love with the place, like so many had before her. No one could actually say what it was, but it captured the hearts of so many people.

Her life had been stressful for a long time before the gun shooting incident when she was playing the role of a drug addict and living rough. The job had taken its toll on her, even before she'd been seriously injured. When she thought about it now, it was only having Babis beside her through everything that kept her going and prevented her from giving up.

She had heard from many people that Kefalos would work its magic and heal her, both physically and mentally, and now she began to believe it for herself.

When she got out of bed every day, she would open the window blind and the sun would come flooding in. The sweet scents of all the garden flowers filled her senses and gave her such joy, along with hope of a new life, better than her previous one.

She hadn't made a decision about working in Kefalos as yet, although she thought the job would be an ideal one for her. She had no family to turn to for advice, but knew that Babis was extremely keen for her to come and live here on the island which he loved, and that she had now come to love.

As she wandered into the village, she thought about all of Babis' relations. He had a wonderful extended family, and the majority of his mother, Mia's family, lived here in Kefalos, either above the village or nearby.

She had spent a lot of time with them, and they were all keen to tell her what had actually brought them to Kefalos and how it was the best thing they'd ever done. Poppy loved sitting with them, whilst listening to their stories.

Babis had been so attentive, always checking she was okay and not getting overtired or experiencing any problems with her injury. She knew he cared for her but still wondered if it was guilt that she had got hurt, and that he had been unable to protect her.

They found it a little awkward to be with each other, yet she felt that, despite his caring ways, he was holding something back. She hoped and wished that he would just sweep her off her feet, carry her to bed and make love to her. She wanted this so much, but how could she make him understand this?

Today they were spending time together and had begun walking down the road leading to the resort. They reached the steps that were a shortcut, rather than staying on the winding road.

Babis held her hand to steady her down the steep flight of steps which were uneven in height and width, so each step had to be navigated differently. When they were both safely down at the bottom, he released her hand from his firm grip. Gently she pushed her hand back into his. He looked at her and frowned, so she looked back into his eyes and smiled.

"Shall we go to the house where I'm staying?" she asked, but then blushed, realising how forward it sounded. Babis looked a little puzzled as Poppy continued. "We're both adults, aren't we, and consenting adults at that. Why don't we go and see what develops?"

They walked together to the little house which had once been Mia's home when she'd first come to the island. It was so traditionally Greek, with its white walls and blue door and shutters.

Poppy's heart was beating fast. Could this be the right time to take their relationship to the next level? She fumbled with the key but finally opened the door, and Babis followed her inside.

Although they had feigned intimacy in their undercover roles, it was now completely different. They'd been focused on their acting role to make everyone believe they were a couple, but here alone in Poppy's house, it felt really strange.

They sat on the long couch, barely touching each other. Babis stretched his arm out along the back of the couch and let his hand drop, almost, but not quite resting on her shoulders. Poppy turned and gazed into his eyes, knowing he cared for her very much.

She'd been told how he continually sat by her bedside, day and night while she was unconscious. He had held her hand and talked quietly to her with a soft and gentle voice, but now they were both a little tongue tied.

"This is crazy," said Babis. "I've had you in my arms so many times and I have kissed you, but now I want to do it, not because I have to, but because I want to." Poppy stood and walked out of the room. Babis wondered if he'd said the wrong thing.

She pulled down the blinds in the bedroom and beckoned him to join her. However, Babis was unsure if he should.

"You have seemed very nervous today, Babis," she commented, as she sat on the edge of the bed and patted the space next to her invitingly.

"I've had a lot on my mind," he said. "I needed some questions answered and you bringing me here, well, its wrong footed me a little. I knew what I wanted to ask, but now I'm not so sure."

"What questions do you need answers to?" Poppy asked, confused.

He gulped before he answered and he felt very stupid. Poppy had never seen him so unsure of himself She smiled and nodded, encouraging him to ask his question.

"Do you think you would ever consider living here?" he questioned her.

"You know I love it here, and yes, I would consider it," Poppy replied. Babis stuttered a little and began again.

"Do you think you could make Kefalos your home forever?" he asked quietly.

" Maybe I could, that depends," Poppy told him.

"Depends on what?" Babis queried, sounding somewhat exasperated.

"On you," she informed him.

"Well, maybe my next question will make things a little clearer. Poppy, we have been through so much already and when you were critically ill, it made me realise that I didn't want to live without you, and I wondered if maybe you might feel the same way?" He looked straight at her.

"Please Babis, ask me the question you are struggling to ask," she pleaded. She looked at him and watched him take a deep breath.

"Poppy, will you marry me?" he finally plucked up the courage to blurt out.

"I thought you would never ask," she smiled, gazing into his eyes. "Yes, I would love to marry you."

"This makes me so very happy," Babis almost laughed in relief, with all his pent up nervousness being released from his body as if a pressure valve had been switched off. He moved close and wrapped his arms around her. He then kissed her like he'd never kissed her, or anyone before.

His heart was racing as he moved next to her. She moved closer to him and his big strong arms engulfed her. He held her face close to his and smiled as he began to kiss her over and over again. Poppy snuggled into him, her breathing becoming slow and measured. This is what they'd wanted for so long.

It was a few minutes later that Babis lifted her body. It felt so frail. Even though she was well on the way to a full recovery, she still seemed vulnerable to him. He gently laid her down on the bed and she smiled up at him, which was her way of giving consent to Babis.

Poppy felt safe and secure with him, and knew he would never hurt her. She also knew that, if she was honest, she'd been attracted to him from the first day they'd met. She also knew that what was about to happen next was inevitable.

She lifted her arms up to allow Babis to remove her loose fitting top, revealing a pretty lace edged bra. He sighed heavily, liking what he was seeing. Excited now, he couldn't believe what was about to happen. He tentatively and gently cupped her breasts in his large hands. She let out a soft moan and snuggled closer to him. Within minutes, their clothes lay strewn across the floor. Their naked bodies were entwined, with them both excited and ready for the next move.

They'd both waited so long for this moment. Poppy couldn't believe the feeling that was pulsating through her body, the release of all their pent-up feelings, their ultimate desire for each other, their willingness to give their love to each other were the only things that mattered to them in that wonderful moment.

Their love making was soft, gentle and prolonged, each exploring the others body. Poppy played with the dark hair on his chest, he too was beginning to regain the athletic body he had before he took on the role of a down and out. Babis hated neglecting his body, and had spent hours at the gym redefining his muscular frame.

Poppy's tiny frame worried him. He felt that his clumsy approach would snap her in two. Now they rested in each other's arms, quite content to remain without the need for words. They knew their relationship had reached a new level, and as they were no longer working together they could be themselves without any problems.

Now Babis had finally asked Poppy to marry him, her happiness was complete. She knew his mothers would help her to prepare for her wedding, and that in true Greek style all the extended family would be involved.

They became her surrogate family, although she was sad that her real parents wouldn't be there to see her get married, as they'd tragically been killed on the day of her graduation ceremony. However, she knew that she had been accepted by all the relations of Babis, and she now felt just like a member of his family.

Babis spent time with Sam between his new shifts, and introduced him to people of his own age who lived in the village.

No one was told about his history or lifestyle, just that he'd come to live here in Kefalos with members of his extended family. Although they were now learning to trust Sam, Mia and Sophia watched him like hawks in case he relapsed, but day by day as they grew to love him, they relaxed their hold on him and allowed him to find his own way in the world.

He still had regular meetings with his mentor, and the follow up reports were always very positive. Mia and Sophia knew that once addiction had taken hold it would never leave, but it was possible to control it rather than give way to it.

Sam looked very much like his half-brother, and very soon he was recognised as a member of the Kefalos community. At first, he was hesitant to make new acquaintances, but now he had a few close friends who he spent time with.

One day he asked to speak to Mia and Sophia and they wondered what was wrong. They went up to his room and both waited for him to speak.

"It's hard for me to find the right words to say to you both," Sam began. "You welcomed me warmly into your home, even though you were aware of my past. You never judged me, but you were always there to watch over me and support me, right from the first day I arrived here.

My brother and you two have taught me what a real family is. It isn't someone who uses you to their own ends, or expects you to do whatever they ask. In the past I have scavenged for food, day after day, when my mother had spent what little money we had on her addiction.

She used the addiction she'd created in my body to make me do unspeakable things, with no remorse whatsoever. You have never done that, you have only given me love, the like of which I have never known before."

The two girls were almost in tears now as they listened.

"Saying thank you can be an empty phrase, if your actions don't show you're really thankful. From this day forward, I want to make you proud of me. I have sunk to unimaginable levels of humanity, but now I see the world can be a much better, caring place, than the one I used to live in. I now have food to eat and a place to sleep, that is both clean and secure, and I have clean clothes and a desire to be smart.

Part of my rehab programme was to make amends to the people I have hurt or harmed in some way. I have no mother or father to make amends to, but I am lucky to have a caring older brother who has loved me and taken me from the depths of depravity and accepted me. You two have treated me as your own son, for which I am extremely grateful. I would love to be that son and I want, by my actions, to repay you for the life you have given me and the love you always show to me.

I also want Babis to be proud of me. I want to study to become a carer for other addicts and try to give back what has been given to me."

Mia and Sophia took turns in hugging Sam. They now knew what he really wanted to do with his new life, and they also knew what they needed to do, knowing they would always be there to support him.

CHAPTER 10
KALI'S QUEST

Kali was now working for a firm of solicitors in Kos town. She loved her role, which was mostly investigation based. A lot of her time was spent locating relatives named in wills. She'd spoken to the manager of her firm, who had agreed that she could also open a case in an effort to find any details of Sam's family members. This investigation had become a priority for Kali, now that her mothers' wanted to formally adopt Sam.

It would appear that his birth had never been registered, so she had no real starting point. She tried to find information using the details she had of Sam's birth mother, but was uncertain whether the name she'd been given was her actual birth name, so it was going to be a very challenging task.

She went to the paediatric centre in the village where members of her family worked, and they were happy to help.

"Do you have any information regarding the mother who abandoned her son here, all those years ago?" Kali asked the family.

They searched the records to find that an unknown elderly woman had walked into the centre carrying a small baby. She'd entered the 'Ladies Toilet' and was seen on the CCTV carrying a baby, but exited without the child.

She was seen leaving the main entrance and getting into a battered old car and driving off. They concluded that this woman was too old to have given birth to the child. There had followed an intensive search to locate the woman, but she was never found.

Kali wondered who this woman was, and if she, perhaps, still lived in the village which she was about to visit next.

She visited a place on the island where people had told her the woman last lived. She was horrified when she finally found the hovel that had been not only her home, but Sam's too.

It was in a tiny village, and when she questioned people there, they were loath to answer any questions. The woman was an embarrassment to the village, conducting herself as she did. Others said they kept well away from her, as she was nothing but a prostitute, regularly taking men into her home day and night.

Even after her little baby boy was born, she still carried on plying her trade. It seemed that no one from the village had ever been in her house. They said she'd moved away, possibly off the island some time ago.

"And good riddance to her!" the locals all said.

Kali explained that she had died and they were trying to find any living relative, especially the father of the abandoned baby.

"Good luck with that!" one woman laughed with scorn, when Kali said this.

"He could be one of many, many men," another woman told Kali.

This had been a depressingly unsuccessful visit, as Kali had not discovered anything at all. She knew that most women from the island would go to Rhodes or Athens to have their babies, but some did deliver here on the island. Maybe there would be some records at the hospital.

Kali made an appointment to see the records clerk at the hospital, where she would explain exactly what she was trying to discover.

"When was the baby actually born?" the clerk asked.

"I'm not sure," Kali admitted.

"How old is he now?" the clerk went on to ask.

"He doesn't know exactly," Kali replied. The clerk looked at her in disbelief.

"Was he born on Kos?" she asked.

"Maybe," said Kali, already deciding she wasn't going to get anywhere with this enquiry.

"I have records on the data base which show births here at the hospital," the clerk instructed. "However, without a year of birth, you could be searching forever."

Although she felt like this was a complete waste of her time, Kali thanked the clerk and asked if she could make another appointment, "should I uncover any more information."

"Of course you can," the clerk said smiling, but Kali could see she didn't particularly relish the thought of searching through old records, and how could her parents apply to adopt Sam if there were no documents to confirm his existence?

Days later when she had again been asking the same questions, having explained what she knew so far, an older woman came forward.

"Have you asked at the gipsy camp? They might know something," the woman suggested. "There is a woman there who helps with birthing."

"Where is this camp?" Kali asked the woman.

After being given directions, she drove to the location of the camp, driving down the unmade road that led to a clearing in the tall trees. There were wooden huts made from pallets, some being used as homes, others holding animals. There were also a few battered caravans and old vehicles scattered about here and there. At the far end was a heap of scrap metal and old fridges, along with broken down air conditioning units.

Kali would regularly see these vehicles collecting scrap in her own village, the owner using a battered megaphone to let people know they were collecting in her area. She'd often wondered where it ended up, and now she knew.

As she approached the site, she could see numerous children playing. Two men came from the caravans to ask what she was doing. They were highly suspicious of anyone who came to their homes.

Kali explained what she was trying to find out, but they didn't look impressed. One of the men whispered something to the other. Kali felt a little nervous being here on her own, especially with no one knowing where she was. She needn't have been, as the older of the two men gestured to Kali to follow him.

An old woman was sitting by a fire. The man spoke quietly to her and she looked up at Kali.

"Cross her palm with silver and she will try and help you," the man announced.

Kali was surprised at this request, but fumbled in her handbag and took out a twenty euro note. The woman took it from her and placed it into her pocket, but gave her no change.

"Now you may ask your question," the woman said to Kali. The man walked away, now satisfied that Kali had paid the price for information.

Kali spoke about Sam's mother, about how she was a drug addict who had abandoned her older son at the centre in Kefalos several years before. She spoke of the woman's younger son, who was now in Kefalos, and how they were trying to discover as much as they could.

"Why?" asked the old woman suspiciously.

"Because my family want to adopt him," Kali informed her. "He's all alone in the world."

"Why is he alone?" the woman questioned.

"Because his mother has died," Kali told her.

"Did she live near here?" the old woman asked.

"We think so. She lived in the village over there" Kali replied, pointing in the direction of their home. "They told me that sometimes women came here to give birth and you helped them," Kali stated, "if they couldn't afford, or didn't want to go anywhere else because of their circumstances."

"So, you think maybe she came here twice?" the old woman asked.

"Maybe, we aren't really sure," Kali told her. The old woman looked deep in thought.

"Perhaps she did come, it could have been her. Two boys you say?" the woman queried. Kali nodded an affirmative.

"But the first one was so long ago."

"Yes, more than twenty years."

"The second child?" she asked.

"About fifteen years, perhaps."

"And they were from the village over yonder?"

"We think so."

"She gave me a name but I don't know if it was her real name," the woman divulged. "She said her name was Maria."

Kali sat bolt upright. That was the name that she'd been told, but being such a common name here on the island, she thought it was not important in her search.

"And she went back to the village?"

"For a time, we believe," Kali agreed.

"She was a woman on her own, with no man to support her," the woman said, and then stunned Kali when she added. "She gave away the first child."

"Yes, that's right," Kali said, with hope now in her voice.

"But she kept the other and he lived in the village with her?"

"Yes," Kali accepted.

"She was not a good clean woman. She was a bad mother and men paid her."

"Yes, that was her."

"I helped her give birth. She paid me for the help. I am sorry I know nothing more than what you already know."

Kali looked deflated. It seemed to have been going so well. The best lead she'd had so far.

110

"Because I have given you nothing, I will tell your fortune for you," the woman offered.

"It's okay," Kali reacted. "What you have told me has helped me form a picture of her life."

"But it's not right for me to accept your money," she said.

The old woman fumbled around in her pocket to retrieve the note, which she then attempted to return to Kali.

"No, it's okay. Keep it," Kali said.

"Then I must read for you," the woman almost demanded. She took a pack of dog-eared cards out of her other pocket and asked Kali to shuffle them. Kali took them from her but almost dropped them she felt so nervous. Having shuffled them with difficulty she handed them back to the woman, who began to place them one by one on an old wooden table next to her. She then began the reading.

"I see two women from different backgrounds. Neither has a man, although they are strong together. I feel much love for their daughter who doesn't know her father, and a son who came to them later, a good boy, a strong boy, a boy who broke their hearts." Kali tried not to react.

"He went away but has now returned. Nothing is as it seems. He is a good man and not, as many chose to believe, a bad man. He will bring another blessing to his family. All of this is the question you are asking with your heart. Have hope.

And you, my dear, you do not have a sweetheart and you have not shared your body with any man."

Kali blushed when hearing this. At her age, many of her friends had been married and had children of their own. She listened as the woman continued with the reading.

"Whilst you search for answers to the riddle before you, you will meet a man, although not from these shores. He will help you in the challenge you have to fulfil. He will enter your heart and will enter your body, and you will forever be as one.

He will give you two surprise blessings. This is meant to be. It has already been written in your stars." The old woman closed her eyes as if searching for further information.

"Thank you," Kali said, thinking the woman had finished, but no.

"Go to the church of St Stephanos, light a candle and ask for his help. He will guide you." The old woman looked straight at Kali. "Go now, go quickly. Do not return here again. There is nothing here to help you – Go!"

Kali stood abruptly and held out her hand to the old woman who muttered something that Kali could not hear, and then she also stood and turned away from Kali and walked away. Kali was dumbfounded by everything that had just been said, and how it had been put to her.

She returned to her car and drove away swiftly. As she drove home she tried to assimilate the information the old woman had given her. It was sparse and Kali wondered if any of it was of any real help. At least she now felt that the real mother of Babis and Sam had been there.

It seemed all progress in the search had come to a standstill. Kali attempted to compose a letter to the relevant authorities to explain that no evidence could be found regarding a registration of the birth of Sam. Following extensive investigations, no father was known, and the woman who was his birth mother was no longer alive. Therefore, she was asking for permission to put in, on behalf of her mothers, a request to formally adopt Sam as their son. Sadly, she received no reply, or acknowledgment of her request.

She began to lose the motivation and enthusiasm she had commenced the search with. Although she did not want to let her mothers' down, all her hard work now seemed to have amounted to nothing.

CHAPTER 11
LOVE IS IN THE AIR

It was time for Kali's annual review at the firm where she worked. They had been very supportive of her quest, as long as she continued to fulfil the requirements of her job. They were pleased with her, and congratulated her on her hard work. They understood the disappointment she felt at not solving the problem around Sam's proposed adoption. They felt she should be commended for all that she had brought to the firm.

She was now going to be introduced to a new member of the team, a man who'd moved to the company from abroad. In walked a good-looking man, who promptly offered his hand to Kali. She shook his hand and looked at him as he smiled at her. Her heart gave a jump and skipped a beat. He had such an infectious smile that she found herself smiling back at him, but then blushed profusely. However, it wasn't until he spoke that she actually went weak at the knees.

"I am pleased to meet you. I have heard a lot about you," he said, speaking in a velvety smooth, hypnotic French accent.

"I have heard nothing about you," she quietly replied, but then realised she'd said it out loud.

"I am sure you will soon get to know all about me," he said with a smile in his voice.

'I hope so,' she thought, happy that this time she hadn't said it aloud. The mysterious Frenchman kept coming into her thoughts as she drove home.

The next day when she was getting ready to go to work, she wondered if the mystery man would be there again today. She hoped so, so much so that she got butterflies in her stomach! When she arrived at work, the reason for her butterflies was already there waiting, sitting at the desk opposite hers.

"Bonjour Kaliee," he said, elongating her name.

"Bonjour," she replied, but then added. "Sorry, I don't know your name."

"I am Jacques," he told her, with a voice that could melt chocolate from twenty paces!

"Well then, Bonjour Jacques," she said, trying to copy his pronunciation. They both laughed at this.

"Tell me about you," he suggested.

"I am the daughter of two parents, both female, one Greek and the other is English," Kali informed this new man. "I have an adopted brother and I have lived in Kefalos all my life."

"And what do you do for pleasure?" Jacques questioned. Kali's cheeks glowed a little at this question, and she faltered a little as she replied.

"I like to spend time on the beach and I love to swim in the sea. I like spending time with my crazy Greek family, and I love my job," she informed the man sitting opposite.

"And this is your only pleasure?" Kali stared at the floor. She didn't know how to respond as he continued to question her. "Do you not enjoy good food and fine wine? Do you like the theatre, or do you enjoy dancing?"

Although she liked home cooked food and the occasional glass of wine or spirit, she simply could not agree that it gave her the same pleasure as watching the movement of the ocean, or simply bathing in the sea.

"You must show me why you like the beach. I have always lived in the city, where trips to the sea were infrequent. Maybe we could go at the weekend and you can show me your favourite beach."

Kali couldn't believe her ears. Was this man offering her a date? Don't be silly she told herself. "Of course," she however replied to Jacques, in her mind already surrendering to him!

"It's a date then," he smiled. He then walked to the door where he stopped, turned around and looked back at her. "I am out of the office today and Friday. Shall we say six o'clock Saturday evening for my first introduction to the magic of the sea?"

'Grab your coat girl, you've pulled!' Kali thought, smiling to herself like a grinning Cheshire cat. "Bring your swimwear and a towel. We can't visit the beach without a dip in the sea."

"Understood," he said. After curiously saluting her, he was gone.

Kali sat at her desk and took a few deep breaths. Was this really happening? She got on with her work, but every so often she felt butterflies in her stomach, as she thought about the forthcoming weekend ahead.

She had half the contents of her wardrobe on the bed that afternoon as her mother, Sophia, walked in. "Having a clear out?" she asked.

"Not really, I'm just looking for something to wear," Kali told her mother.

"What for?" her mum questioned.

"Just for the beach," Kali replied.

"For the beach," Sophia laughed. "Wear what you normally wear?"

"That won't do today, Mum," Kali admitted.

"And why not?" Sophia asked her daughter, but then questioned. "What's this all about, or should I say, who is this all about?" hearing this, Kali smiled at her mum.

"I'm taking a colleague from work to see the beach at Volcania," she announced.

"You're taking a colleague from work?" Sophia interrogated, obviously intrigued.

"Okay, a good-looking Frenchman has come to work at my office, and I have agreed to show him the beach," Kali stated.

"Ah," Sophia said knowingly. "And you like this guy?"

"Stop it Mum," Kali pleaded.

"Okay, put on a black full body swimsuit. Don't show too much, and put that lovely Kaftan over it. You will look stunning and you will capture his heart, as I think he is capturing yours."

"Thanks Mum," Kali blushed. She blushed so easily these days and had no control over it.

"Let me tell you something," Sophia said. "I knew your mother, Mia, was the one for me from the very first time I ever saw her, and she told me she felt the same. Love doesn't have any time limits, it just happens. Kali, go and discover if he is the one for you. You have mine and Mia's blessings." Oh, how Kali loved her two mums.

Kali had arranged to meet Jacques in the car park on the sea front. She was early, so parked her little Fiat and waited eagerly, but a little anxiously, for him to arrive. A large white Mercedes, four by four, pulled into the car park and stopped close by.

'Nice car,' she thought, but then suddenly realised it was Jacques in the driver's seat.

Suddenly she had a dilemma, should she invite him to travel in her car, or wait to be asked for the offer of being a passenger in his? Her question was answered when Jacques opened the door and spotted Kali in her car. He walked across and peered in through the open window.

"Bonsoir Kaliee." Oh how she loved the way he said her name. "I think my legs are a little long for your car," he laughed. "Would you care to join me in mine?"

"Of course," was all she could muster as she climbed out of her Fiat, remembering at the last minute to grab her beach bag.

"You look nice," Jacques said, making her go weak at the knees.

"You are the second person to tell me that today," she revealed.

"So I have a rival for your affections, do I?" he laughed.

"Only my mum," Kali said, smiling at him.

"I see," Jacques offered. He opened the car door and Kali climbed inside.

"Where to my lady?" he joked.

"Take the main road out towards Ikos and carry straight on," she said.

"Understood," he replied.

As they came close to Kali's more usual beach, she told Jacques to turn left towards the winery. "I'm afraid the road is not good here. I would hate for your car to get damaged."

"It's made for bad roads," he observed.

They passed the entrance to the winery and here the road got quite bad, with large ruts and even bigger potholes, but the car navigated them all with ease. Kali thought of how her little Fiat would have rattled and almost groaned going down this road, but the Mercedes was simply laughing at these conditions!

She knew the beach here would be quiet at this time of day, unlike Kochylari, where the kite surfers would often go to in the late afternoon.

They came to the car park and Jacques stopped the car. "Are you ready for an invigorating dip?" Kali asked.

"Please, lead on," he said, gesturing that he would follow her.

Jacques was very impressed with the beach, with its lovely soft white sand, along with only a few wooden umbrellas and sun loungers. Although the waves were quite gentle now, Kali knew the wind could quickly get up and change the sea completely.

She put her bag on a sunbed and Jacques did the same. There was a pregnant pause, as both prepared to remove their outer garments ready to go in the sea. Kali had listened to her mum and had chosen to wear a full bodied swimming costume, and not her customary tiny bikini.

As she removed her Kaftan, Jacques looked on with approval. He then removed his shirt and shorts and it was her turn to be impressed.

"Well then," she said, feeling a little embarrassed and lost for words.

Jacques broke the tension by shouting, "Last one in pays for dinner."

They ran into the sea like two naughty school kids, splashing each other as they entered. Enjoying the cool water, they stayed in a little while longer than intended.

"Enough now," Jacques remarked, "or I will be all wrinkly."

Kali looked at him more closely now. He had a good body, but it was his easy way and his lovely 'winning' smile that really attracted her. They each pulled out their towels and began to dry off.

"One moment," Jacques said and went to his car. He returned with a cool bag, which he unloaded onto the sunbed.

"Bread, cheese and red wine; a perfect French treat," Jacques smiled.

As they feasted on the picnic, the sun began to go down. "Now you will see the beauty of the sea," Kali informed him.

The sky was red and blood orange, which perfectly reflected in the still water. The red ball of the sun descended slowly into the horizon, perching momentarily before sinking into the ocean.

Neither had spoken whilst they were watching the end of the day and the beginning of the evening, giving nature centre stage and gazing wistfully out to sea.

"Magnifique," Jacques whispered eventually. "Truly beautiful," he said gazing at Kali, although she didn't see him.

The darkness came swiftly after the sun had gone down.

"Shall we go now?" Jacques asked.

"Perhaps we should," Kali said reluctantly, whilst savouring every moment with Jacques.

They climbed into the car, although not quite dry from the swim. Jacques drove carefully down the rutted lane back to the main road. It was still relatively early, but Jacques said he had to be at the airport to fly to Athens on the early morning flight.

When they arrived back at the car park, Jacques jumped out and opened the door for Kali. She walked to her car and put the key in the door, but turned to find that Jacques was standing right behind her. Without hesitation, he wrapped his arms around her and kissed her. She went weak at the knees. She had not expected this! When he finally released her, she felt so lightheaded that she almost stumbled.

"Thank you so much Kaliee. Being here with you today has been wonderful." Kali thought so too, as Jacques said. "I will see you when I return soon from Athens."

"Okay," she managed to say, as she climbed into her car.

They both drove off in separate cars, both with emotions running amok. This was all happening so fast, yet that didn't make it wrong.

All the way, as she journeyed home, Kali did not lose the smile now permanently etched upon her face.

The office seemed empty without Jacques. He'd now been away for several weeks, and Kali wondered if he would ever come back. She had feelings like she'd never experienced before.

She was no longer content, and did not get the same pleasure from her early morning swims as before. She remembered how much fun she'd had with Jacques, when they'd spent that evening in the sea at Volcania beach. In fact, she avoided going there now and went to Lagada instead, where there was more going on for her to watch.

Happiness eluded her for the first time in her life, so she threw herself into her work. Her colleagues could see she was no longer her normal, bubbly self, and it worried them. All this discontent because of one evening with a guy she knew very little about, but who had stirred such strong emotions within her.

Mia and Sophia could tell something was wrong, but as she hadn't confided in them, they didn't question her.

Life went on, with long hot sunny days that brought many tourists to the resort, often ones that had been visitors to the island year in year out, and called it their second home.

Kali had always felt blessed with the life she had, but for the first time she now felt loneliness, as if a part of her was missing. Perhaps Jacques had decided that the job here wasn't for him, after all, she knew nothing about him, He could have a girlfriend, or dare she think, perhaps even a wife that he had not told her about. However, the kiss they'd shared had so much love and emotion in it, she just couldn't let go of the feeling that Jacques was the one for her.

Jacques was a little older than Kali, although she didn't know his age exactly. He'd moved to the island from France, where he worked for the sister company, although she was unsure of what position he had held within it. He was just a normal guy, no arrogance, no superiority, just one of the team. Although she'd only known him a short time, she was really missing him.

She walked into the office quite early in the morning and sat at her desk. To her immense surprise, as she looked around she saw that, sitting next to her was Jacques. She wanted to run to him and hug him, but she knew she shouldn't. He smiled the most beautiful smile, indicating that he was also pleased to see her too.

"Hey," he said. "I've missed you."

Kali's heart beat like a tightened drum. Should she admit that she'd really missed him? 'No, stay cool,' she told herself.

"You've been gone for a while," she mentioned.

"I know," Jacques replied. "It wasn't my intention to be away so long, but I met with a few complications that I had to deal with before I could return."

'Complications,' Kali had the thought again, 'perhaps a wife and children? Don't go there,' she ordered herself.

"I need to talk to you," Jacques said.

'Here it comes.' she thought.

"Are you free for lunch?" he enquired.

"Yes, I believe so," Kali replied.

"Shall we say one o'clock?" Jacques suggested.

"One o'clock it is," Kali confirmed.

She sat there with all sorts of thoughts running through her head, finding it difficult to concentrate on her work for the rest of that morning. She just went over and over in her head what Jacques might want to discuss with her. When the time came, her nerves were completely on edge when Jacques came into her office.

"Ready?" he asked.

"Yes," Kali replied, although hesitantly.

"Okay, let's walk down to 'Ficus' and have something to eat. I've noticed that it's quiet at this time of the day," Jacques suggested.

"My friend owns that restaurant," Kali observed.

"Is it a problem?" he asked.

"No, not really," she lied, not sure if she wanted her friends to see her with Jacques.

Tilly, one of Mia's long-time friends, had told her that her daughter, Maria's extended family had planned to refurbish an old restaurant and to run it together as a business. Mia was delighted for her friend, and offered to help in any way needed.

The work continued all through the winter, removing all the old exterior wood canopies and constructing new pergolas. The original separated bar and restaurant were now joined together, with a long bar at one side and terraces for tables at the other.

Tilly had always been very creative and she put forward her designs for the decor, using bamboo as a facia for the bar and for the roofs of the pergolas. Subtle grey floor tiles were put down, and glass concertina doors were fitted so that in inclement weather, or during the winter, indoor dining could still take place. Every time she walked, or drove past, Mia would take in how the building work had progressed.

Finally, at the start of the season, all the building works and decorations were completed and it looked fabulous. Menus were printed, the bar was stocked and everything seemed about ready for the opening.

Mia and Sophia were invited to the first night's opening, as was Kali, as she'd been friends with, and had attended school with Maria.

The atmosphere was wonderful and the food was fabulous. Keeping it all in the family, Maria's husband was the chef in charge of the kitchen; Maria was the head waitress, whilst Tilly's son was in charge of the bar.

Mia watched as Tilly greeted people and showed them to their seats. She'd always worked as either a waitress or in 'Public Relations' since her move to Kefalos many years earlier, and she was so good at it. Her customer service was second to none.

The restaurant, which was given the new name of Ficus, became a fabulous success. It was full to bursting most evenings, with the staff always being run off their feet. It received great feedback and was the place to go to that summer.

Mia was so pleased for Tilly and her family. It was here that became Mia's favourite place for coffee, and she would go there on a few mornings every week. She and Tilly had been through various traumas during their friendship, and were always there to support each other.

"Are you embarrassed to be seen with me?" Jacques asked her inquisitively.

"My God, no," she hastily replied, but then blushed, which made Jacques smile.

They walked down to the resort and went into Ficus. Tilly, her mum's friend, came to greet Kali and Jacques. She raised her eyebrows at Kali as if about to question her.

"This is Jacques," Kali informed her. "He works at the office with me."

Tilly gave her a knowing nod and then directed them to a table at the far end of the restaurant, a much sought after table with the best views, truly a quality spot. Tilly handed them the menus and left them to decide on their order.

"Would you like anything to drink?" Tilly questioned.

"Just a water, please," Jacques requested.

"I'll have the same," Kali agreed.

After Tilly had left them alone, Jacques began to tell his story to Kali.

"Well now, let me explain about my absence," he began.

"You don't need to," Kali replied.

"Oh yes I do," Jacques said. "Originally I went over to the French office to settle some of my accounts. Whilst there, I was told a buyer had been found for my house. Once I'd closed the sale and handed my French work over to a colleague, I came back and secured a property in Greece, where I intend to live."

"In Greece," Kali said, with her hopes and spirits taking a dive.

"Yes," he confirmed, but then questioned her, "I see you look disappointed."

"You said Greece," an unsure kali queried. "Do you mean you intend to live there and work out of the Athens office?"

"I hope not, I would have to travel by plane every day." Kali looked at him and he smiled. "I have bought a house in Kefalos, at the back of the village. I believe a lot of your family have properties there." Kali, now excited, couldn't quite take it in. Jacques was going to live in Kefalos.

He went on to tell her, "I fell in love with Kefalos when I came here years ago to open the local office. It has always been my intention to move here, once all the offices were functioning properly." Kali couldn't believe what she was hearing, as he continued.

"I would like to tell you a little about myself. What you see is what you get," he smiled. "I know I'm a few years older than you. I've never been married, although I came close once. I love my work and I have dedicated time and money to making my company a profitable business."

"Your company," Kali was mystified. "Your company?" she said again.

"Yes, I own this firm, also the one in France and in Athens. I have good staff who work for me and whom I can trust. I spent a lot of my younger years working every hour available to me to build up the business, and therefore missed out on lots of leisure activities and having fun.

When I went with you to the beach that evening, it was such fun, and I realised what was missing in my life. I now want to have even more fun and hope that you will be able to help me appreciate all of the other things that I have been missing, like enjoying beautiful sunsets, experiencing quality time, and not working all the time.

I don't mind admitting that you have swept me off my feet, which have until now been firmly set on the ground whilst trying to be a good businessman. You have, in the short amount of time I've known you, completely changed what I want in life."

Kali was trembling at his words. "I would love to spend time with you but…" she began. Jacques looked a little disappointed as Kali continued. "I really would like to spend time with you; however, I have a task which I need to complete, and it could take some time."

Jacques looked a little deflated. Was this just an excuse? Perhaps Kali didn't want this relationship to go any further.

"I understand, and won't push you," he told her.

"No, no, no," Kali pleaded. "I want you to push me. I would really love to spend more time with you. I was hoping to have completed this task a long time ago. I would like to tell you about it, as it concerns all my family." Kali then began to explain it all to Jacques.

"My brother Babis, who was adopted at birth, had been working away. During that time he discovered he had a half-brother. His birth mother died some time previously, and Babis was now his only relative.

His name is Sam and he now lives with my mothers. He was a drug addict who'd been used and abused by his birth mother, who was also an addict and a dealer herself.

As he has no family, my parents would like to adopt him. I know that sounds relatively easy, however, he has no birth certificate and is not sure where he was born. He has no idea how old he is or when he was actually born. I have been trying to find these details for him so an adoption could go ahead, but so far, I've been unsuccessful.

I cannot let my mothers' down and need to sort this for them. This is ruling my life at the moment, so this is why I cannot commit to anything else until this is sorted. I'm sorry, Jacques."

As Kali paused for breath, Jacques could hear the emotion in her voice as he listened intently to the story without interrupting. When Kali finally finished, he smiled at her.

"Kali," he began, "Will you let me help you? That way, we could spend time together and get to know each other. I am sure we can put our heads together and come up with the solution to this problem. You will have to share with me all you know. That is, or course, if you trust me with this information." When Kali looked at him and saw the honesty in his face, she smiled and nodded.

"It's time we were back at the office," she said, "or I will be getting sacked!"

"Not if you're here with the top man," he laughed. "In fact, take the day off and come and look at my new house. I could do with some input from a female, especially a female as beautiful as you."

CHAPTER 12
THE HOUSE THAT JACQUES BUILT

Jacques drove the car through the warren of narrow streets, slowly navigating past parked cars and large flower pots positioned along the road. A few Yiayias' (Greek grandmothers') were chatting in the shade. They looked up inquisitively, as they didn't recognise this shiny white Mercedes SUV and wondered whether it was a tourist or some official visitor, maybe a doctor or a politician?

They passed through the village and journeyed along one of the many roads that led to the outer neighbourhoods, where many large houses and villas had been built. Kali pointed out some of the villas, which belonged to members of her family.

As they travelled further, they came to an unfinished road that led away from the area. Continuing on for a little while along this unmade road they were eventually confronted by a newly completed house. It had neither an obvious plot size nor fence but was stunning, with arched balconies, a red tiled roof and a façade built with local stone.

Kali counted the windows as they approached, five on the first floor at the front, and four at the bottom, with a large double door in the centre. The house faced open land at the front, with no other houses in view.

Jacques drove round to the rear of the property where Kali was quite surprised by the view from there. The land dipped suddenly about six hundred metres from the rear of the property, allowing for the wonderful view of the sea and the island of Kalymnos.

It was beautifully situated out of the village, but not too far out, and once the road was finished it would be easy to drive from here, back to the main road.

Jacques got out of the car and opened the door for Kali. 'Quite the gentleman,' she thought. He took a set of keys from his pocket and promptly opened the front door. There was a large hallway with stairs leading off both to the left and right, natural wood doors led to the two reception rooms and a door at the rear led to the kitchen, or what would be the kitchen, once it had been fully fitted with cupboards and appliances. An archway from the kitchen led to what Kali imagined would be the dining room, with its large patio doors ensuring full vantage of the stunning view.

Kali said nothing. Jacques looked at her from time to time for any reaction, but she gave nothing away.

"Shall we go upstairs?" Jacques asked.

'Well that's a question," she thought, but nodded in agreement.

As they ascended the fantastic staircase which led to a minstrel gallery, with doors leading to what would eventually be bedrooms and bathrooms, Kali could see that at least two of the rooms would have en-suite bathrooms. One room was larger than the other and she guessed this would be the master bedroom, which as she'd previously thought, had its own wet room, Jacuzzi, bath and separate toilet, all in differing shades of grey. 'Fifty Shades of Grey' came into her head, but she dismissed it immediately, as she had heard about the content of that particular novel.

"Well," Jacques said eventually. "Can I have your verdict?"

"It's awesome," she stated. "It has such potential for an interior decorator to show their skills."

"Oh, no, I don't want a stranger to design it. I want someone who knows me to decorate it," he said, to which Kali smiled.

"But I don't know you any more than an interior designer would," she pointed out to Jacques.

"That is why we will spend more time together, so that you do know me," he admitted. "I want to find out what you would like, if it was your own home." Kali didn't know what to say.

"You will have to give me some time," she said eventually. "I have yet to sort out Sam's adoption."

"I told you we will sort it out together," Jacques stated. "I have started to work on it and I have an idea where I can find some information that will help us," Kali grinned at Jacques. She was already getting to like him more and more by the hour.

'Slow down,' she ordered herself.

Grabbing him and hugging him there and then came into her mind, but it was too fast and too soon. She'd only known him a short while, but already felt deeply attracted to him. They walked through the house again, and then returned to the car.

"I'd better get you back to the office before I sack you," he joked, all the time smiling at her. He wondered if this young woman could ever see herself with him in the future, although he didn't want to rush her, as that might spoil everything.

Jacques drove them back to the office, where Kali's colleagues looked questioningly at her as she entered.

"We thought something had happened to you when you didn't come back from lunch," one of her workmates said.

"Kali has been helping me with a small project I've been working on," Jacques said stepping in, in Kali's defence.

They all looked down at their work as the two of them left the foyer and walked towards Kali's room. As they left, Kali looked at Jacques and they both laughed.

"See, this is the fun I'm talking about. We need to have fun together," Jacques announced. Kali felt the butterflies in her stomach.

"Could you give the house some thought? You know colours, soft furnishings, furniture, if you don't mind. I'd like you to accompany me to Athens to start the process of choosing what we both think would be right for our house, sorry, THE house," he quickly corrected himself.

"Now," he continued, "let's get some work done before it's time for you to leave for your home, and if I am not being too presumptuous, can I pick you up at eight-thirty? We can go out to eat together and discuss things further?"

Kali wasn't sure how to reply. "Okay," was all she could manage. Jacques smiled at her. He was now obviously besotted.

"Eight-thirty it is then," he confirmed, as he walked out of the room.

Kali's heart was racing, was this really happening? She'd never met anyone like Jacques before, besides the good looks and the famous French charm; he seemed to be a really nice man. She liked him, feeling desire for the first time in her life, and it felt so good.

She would have to explain to her two mums, although the glow on her cheeks when she returned home was enough for both Mia and Sophia to smile knowingly at each other.

"I'm going for a meal with Jacques," Kali told them.

"Oh, its Jacques now, is it? Not Monsieur?" Mia joked.

"Its business," Kali told them in defence.

"Not monkey business I hope," Mia mocked, with her and Sophia laughing together.

Kali looked stunning in a pale blue shift dress which beautifully showed off her suntanned arms and legs. She styled her hair in loose curls and put on a little makeup. She'd never taken such care getting ready before in her life. She constantly checked herself in the mirror. Was her dress too short, had she put on too much makeup, was this the right handbag to go with the shoes she'd chosen?

Jacques had said eight-thirty, but fifteen minutes early there was a knock on the door. Sophia went to answer.

"Good evening, I am Jacques," he announced. "I have come to collect your daughter, Kali. That is if you are happy for me to take her out?"

"Come in a moment, I would like you to meet Kali's other mum," Sophia said, as he walked through the door. Kali came out of her bedroom and almost floated along the corridor. Jacques gasped when he saw her. She was so beautiful.

Sophia shouted to Mia, who was out on the balcony. As she came through, Jacques caught sight of her. "Your daughter is the image of you," he told Mia.

Mia felt herself blushing. 'My God,' blushing at her age. It was true what Kali had told her, Jacques was a real charmer.

The four of them chatted for a while and Jacques explained how he might be able to help them in their quest for information to facilitate the adoption of Sam. Sophia and Mia were warming to Jacques by the minute. They felt their daughter was in safe hands and were happy for Kali to be going out on a date with him.

As Jacques and Kali left, Mia and Sophia turned to each other and smiled. "We believed in love at first sight when we first met, I think Kali is following in our footsteps," Sophia suggested.

"I hope she will be as lucky as we have been," Mia returned.

They hugged each other. Life had had been good to them, even taking into account what they'd been through with Babis.

Kali and Jacques had spent a lot of time together, both in the office and during evenings and weekends. They still continued to search for information about Sam, although it had so far been a slow and an arduous task.

Working together on Sam's case had brought them even closer, and they had learnt a lot about each other at the same time.

Together they were flying to Athens on a mission to buy furniture and soft furnishings for Jacques' house. She carefully packed her carry-on case, with both casual and evening wear, as Jacques had said he would take her to his favourite restaurant, situated just outside of Athens. She was feeling excited about the trip. Jacques picked her up from her home and the two mums happily waved them off.

The flight was uneventful. After they landed in Athens, they took a taxi to the hotel. Jacques checked them in and the receptionist gave them keys to adjacent rooms. They took the stairs up to the rooms and Jacques left Kali at the door of her room so she could unpack, confirming that he would meet her in the hotel bar for a drink, before they ate in the hotel restaurant.

Kali was getting more and more used to being with Jacques and no longer felt any nerves when in his company. She chatted easily with him during the drinks and meal, and then back at the bar, where they shared a couple of nightcaps.

Jacques excused himself, saying he had to make a couple of phone calls before it was too late, and left Kali after having first arranged a time to meet her in the morning for breakfast.

Kali finished her drink and went up to her room. She was glad of the reasonably early night, as tomorrow they would be visiting many shops and warehouses to try and order what was on their long wish list of potential purchases.

Sleep eluded her at first and she could hear Jacques talking in the room next to her, although she could not make out what he was saying. It was strange to be in the next room to Jacques, and she thought about what it might be like to be in that room with him.

She found him to be very attractive and wondered whether their friendly relationship would develop into something more serious. She hoped it would, as she was certainly ready to take it further! Kali snuggled up to her pillow, hugging it and wishing it was Jacques snuggling up beside her. With these thoughts in her head, she dreamed of what might be.

The next morning, Jacques was waiting at the breakfast table when Kali arrived. Ever the gentleman, he stood up and pulled out the chair for her. Kali thought she couldn't imagine any of the local village boys doing this for her.

After consuming a hearty breakfast, a taxi arrived to take them to the shopping centre in Athens. They spent all morning looking at furniture. It felt very strange to be looking at beds together, and even stranger when the assistant encouraged them both to lie on the bed to see if the mattress was right for them. They both ended up in fits of laughter and giggles, much to the confusion of the young sales girl.

They enjoyed a light lunch and then continued on, examining swatches of fabric to match curtains and cushions, rugs and mats. Kali was really enjoying this, although Jacques quite often took a backseat while Kali lined up material of different colours and shades.

"You have a good eye for colour and design," he told her. "As an old bachelor myself, I have lived mostly with monochrome, a little clinical really."

"You aren't old, "Kali retorted, but then felt stupid. "Come on, we have a lot to do today and my feet are beginning to hurt."

They continued to shop for another couple of hours and then decided that the remainder could be left until the next day.

The table, for their evening meal, had been booked for eight, so they returned to the hotel to freshen up and change their clothes. They walked up to their separate rooms and put their keys in the locks at the same time, opening their respective doors.

"See you soon," Kali whispered.

"Can't wait," Jacques replied.

Kali went into her room and closed the door behind her, leaning against it for a moment. She smiled to herself, savouring the thought of what might lie ahead. She let out a deep sigh and went to prepare for the evening.

Promptly and politely as ever, Jacques knocked on her room door. When Kali opened the door and saw him standing there, she thought he looked fabulous in his black suit and white shirt. He really was a very good-looking man.

Jacques took a step back to admire Kali. Her short little black dress hugged her body, showing her slim frame to perfection. She wore black high heel shoes and a subtle silver necklace with matching bracelet. Jacques could see just how beautiful she was.

He offered his arm to her and Kali put hers through his. It felt so comfortable to them both to be linked together like this.

The taxi was waiting, they stepped inside and were driven to a small restaurant, a Michelin star establishment run by a Frenchman specialising in fine French cuisine. They were seated in a quiet alcove and presented with menus.

"Bonsoir, Jean-Paul," Jacques said to the waiter, who quietly spoke in French with Jacques. Kali could pick up a few words of what was being said, and then the waiter looked directly at her.

"Jacques says he will choose for you, because he wants you to enjoy the best we have on offer," he smiled at her and Kali smiled in acknowledgement to Jean-Paul.

"That is if it's alright with you of course?" Jacques added, looking at Kali.

"I trust you," Kali said smiling.

"I hope so," Jacques added, and winked at her. Butterflies were now clogdancing in her stomach!

The meal was exceptional, with so many exotic flavours and wine chosen to complement each course. Kali found she was enjoying the evening immensely. Once the waiter had removed the last of the plates, he left them to talk. Jacques began the conversation.

"I have a little surprise for you," he told her. Kali looked a little shocked. "Don't be afraid," Jacques continued. As he passed an envelope to her, she hesitated a little. "Please, open it," Jacques requested, eagerly awaiting a response from Kali as to what was in the envelope.

She took out several sheets of paper. There were letters from various solicitors, along with a couple from a Greek government department. Kali was unsure as to what they were.

"Okay," Jacques said. "Look at the last letter."

Kali did as was requested and took out the last letter from the bundle. She read it, half holding her breath, as she waded her way through it. In essence, it told of the law regarding abandoned children who'd never had their birth registered, and also being unaware of their actual date of birth or age.

Kali slowly continued to study the translated transcript, which told of how papers and declarations had been received by the government, and how, based on this information, their legal department had issued a document declaring it had been proved that Sam had been born in Greece approximately fifteen years ago, and he was registered on a certificate in the name of Kapiris-Taylor. Kali couldn't believe what she was reading, as the name on the document was her family name.

"Here is another surprise for you," Jacques announced, as he handed her another document. "I have filed a request on behalf of your mothers' for them to legally adopt Sam, and as far as I'm aware, there shouldn't be any problems pertaining to it."

"Do my mothers' know about this?" she asked, with tears running down her cheeks and a huge lump in her throat.

"I spoke to them last night, after I had confirmation from the Greek government," Jacques confirmed to her.

"And you have done all this for us?" she questioned gratefully.

"No, I have done it for you," he smiled. "I have done this to release you from the burden that was preventing you from moving on," he told her. "I did it because I'm selfish. I want you but I want all of you, and until this was sorted, I couldn't have that."

"Jacques, you're wonderful," she cried. "Let's go back to the hotel now." Jacques settled the bill and the taxi took them back to the hotel.

"Do you want a nightcap?" Jacques asked as they arrived at the reception area.

"No thank you, I think I'm ready for bed," Kali replied.

Jacques looked at her and smiled, hoping he'd read the signs correctly. Was she now free to start a new life with him?

They reached their bedroom doors and Jacques took out his key to open the door to his room. Kali fumbled in her tiny handbag, but was unable to locate her key. She looked up at Jacques, who was watching her intently.

He cocked his head to one side and gestured to his room. Kali smiled, because she knew that if she went to his room, she was fully aware of what would happen. Knowing this, she went willingly into his room, where waiting on the bed was a large bouquet of flowers. Kali laughed.

"You knew," she said, smiling at Jacques.

"I hoped I knew," Jacques replied, smiling back at her.

He walked towards Kali and put his arms gently around her. She looked up at him, and savouring every second they slowly and gently removed each other's clothes and then slipped beneath the sheets.

"Kali, you are so beautiful," he whispered lovingly, as he kissed her again and again.

Jacques was so gentle, knowing this was, perhaps, her first intimate experience he wanted her to remember it forever, just as he would, each and every time they made love in the future,

Time didn't matter, the age difference didn't matter, in fact, nothing mattered. They both lay still after the love making was finished, both fully satisfied and also blissfully happy.

After a period of silence, Jacques said, "Now Kali, you will have to marry me." She smiled, as this was just what she had dreamed of. Now entwined in each other's arms they slept contently.

Kali had slept so soundly that she hadn't heard Jacques get up or leave the room. Neither had she heard him return, complete with a breakfast tray prepared for two. He sat gently on the bed, and as she stirred and began to open her eyes, he smiled at her.

"Good morning, sleepy head," he said with great affection. Kali half hid her face under the sheet which covered her naked body. She could see that Jacques was showered, dressed, and ready for the day.

She didn't know what to say, or how to react. Jacques' lovely smile made her smile too. She stretched her arms out to him and he leant over her and held her face in his hands. He began to kiss her and she returned the kisses with those of her own. Kali held onto him tightly, afraid she was dreaming and might soon wake up.

"Do you want anything?" Jacques asked, with a cheeky glint in his eye.

"Yes, I do," Kali replied. "I want you."

"I brought breakfast," he said.

"Breakfast can wait," she remarked.

"We have to go shopping," he said, feigning an objection to her request.

"Shopping can wait," Kali whispered. "I want you and I want you now." She released her hold on him, and eagerly, Jacques stripped off his clothes and joined Kali back again between the sheets. They pleasured each other for ages, until neither could wait any longer. As Jacques made love to her she reached heights of pleasure which she could never have imagined, or indeed dreamed of before.

Strong coffee and croissants were the late breakfast consumed. Kali gathered her clothes and slipped on a bathrobe after finding her key in the front compartment of her little handbag. Jacques kindly checked to see if the coast was clear, and she scurried back to her own room to shower and dress for the day ahead.

They ordered and bought many things that afternoon, before catching the plane back to Kos. Upon arriving at the airport, they jumped into Jacques' car and he drove her home, where of course the mums' were waiting patiently for them. Jacques declined to come in when Mia and Sophia opened the door. He blew Kali a kiss and drove away.

Mia looked at Sophia, and then they both looked at Kali. They could both see that she was positively glowing. There was a sparkle in her eyes and a confidence in her demeanour.

Kali looked at them and returned the gaze. It was clear that they both knew she had found love. They didn't need to ask her about the trip, they could see their daughter was truly happy and that meant the world to them.

They talked for a little while about what Jacques had done regarding Sam. They told Kali how grateful they were to him, and how happy they were to have sorted things out at last.

"Now go and get some rest," Mia said to her daughter. "You look exhausted and you have work in the morning."

Kali felt like a little girl again, being told to go to bed. She knew that working would be different from now on, given what had happened over the weekend. She hoped there would be no awkwardness with the staff if Jacques said anything. However, on that part, they had nothing to worry about.

Both Kali and Jacques had arrived at work with smiles on their faces, with neither being able to keep their eyes off each other. Everyone knew there was something different between them, and they were happy, because they all loved Kali and all had great respect for their boss.

Jacques spoke to Kali about setting up the house, now that everything they'd ordered was beginning to be delivered from the mainland. He wondered if she would consider reducing her hours at work and spending more time with him at the house. He explained that it would not affect her salary whilst she was doing this. It seemed like a win-win situation to her.

She hadn't been to the house for a couple of weeks, but today she was going with Jacques to wait for the arrival of all the kitchen appliances. Jacques told her the kitchen units had been fitted and the floor tiled in readiness.

When they came to the end of the concreted area of the road out of the village, Kali noticed that there was no longer a bouncy ride and she was surprised to see that the road had been freshly surfaced with Tarmac since her last visit.

As they neared the house, she could see a stone wall being built around the perimeter of the land, and she realised what a large plot the house stood on. It also looked like the land had been prepared in readiness for the garden to be planted.

They arrived at the house and Jacques opened the front door, allowing Kali to step in before him. Some of the rooms had now been painted in the colours she'd chosen, and there were plastic covered pieces of furniture dotted here and there, waiting for rugs and mats to be place on the tiled floors.

Kali loved this so much. Never in her life before had she ever dreamed that she'd be able to furnish a house of this size without any costs imposed upon her. She couldn't stop smiling as she moved from room to room. There was a knock on the door and Jacques went to answer it. It was the delivery man with the electrical appliances, mainly white goods for the kitchen.

"I will supervise this," he shouted to Kali. "If you don't mind, can you see what's arrived upstairs?"

"Of course," she replied.

She climbed the stairs and went directly to the main bedroom, but when she opened the door, the sight of the room took her breath away! A beautiful, very large antique bed took pride of place in the room, with a matching dressing table, chaise longue, chest of drawers and matching bedside tables. It was obvious that these had come from France and that she certainly hadn't ordered them. It said 'Jacques' all over.

A pure white lace bedspread covered the bed, and the curtains at the window were made of the same material. Scattered on the bed, and looking like a scene from the movies, were red rose petals. Kali stood in awe of the beauty and tranquillity of the room. She glanced out of the window to see the delivery truck leaving and wondered where Jacques was. The door opened and in he walked, looking a little coy.

"Do you like it?" he asked her.

"It's stunning," Kali told him.

"Do I have your approval of my taste?" he went on to ask.

"Do you need it? It is your home after all," she replied.

"Okay, let me change the question," he said, pretending to be exasperated by her.

"If this were your bedroom, would you approve of my choice?"

"Not sure," Kali replied.

"And why aren't you sure?" he continued questioning her.

"I would have to try it out first."

"Then go ahead," he announced with no argument, as Kali lay on the bed.

"I'm still not sure," she said with a laugh, teasing him.

"Why not," Jacques asked, raising his eyes to the ceiling.

"Well the lady in the shop said it was vital that we both lay on the bed together to make sure it was the right mattress for both of us," Kali joked.

Jacques realised she was playing games with him and went to lie next to her. The bed seemed enormous and there was a large gap between them.

"Still not sure;" she mocked. "What if we were both to roll over at the same time?" She began to roll over and Jacques did the same. They ended up very close together, looking each other in the eyes.

"Not bad," Kali noted.

"You little minx," Jacques called her, whilst grabbing her tightly. "Now we will see if the bed is right for us."

It was sometime later that they got dressed again. They straightened the bedclothes, both now convinced that the bed was definitely just right for them.

"Kali, you bring such joy and laughter into my life. This house is nothing without you in it," Jacques proclaimed a little later.

"Are you asking me to move in?" Kali questioned.

"No," he said.

"No?" she queried.

"No," he confirmed. "I'm asking you to be my wife."

"Is this a real proposal, or are you just feeling guilty at taking advantage of me twice?" she questioned, although Jacques was certain she was joking.

"Twice," Jacques shouted. "It's been at least five times!"

"It could be six or seven times if we don't get out of here soon," Kali stated. She raced for the door but Jacques stopped her from leaving.

"Have a look in the bedside cabinet," he requested. She went to the right side of the bed and opened the drawer, but it was empty.

"That's not your side of the bed," he told her laughing.

She walked round to the other side of the bed and tentatively pulled the drawer open. Inside was a gold bag with a red ribbon around it containing a small box. Kali looked at Jacques and he nodded for her to open it. Inside, the box contained the most stunningly beautiful, white gold ring, with an enormous solitaire diamond.

"I know you like silver, but wedding and engagement rings should be gold, so this is white gold," he said. Kali was overcome with emotion. The dreams she'd had about Jacques always led to a proposal, but they had been dreams, lost in the light of day.

"Pinch me," Kali requested and Jacques did just that. "Ouch, it is real," she protested.

"You mean the diamond?"

"No I mean what is happening."

"It's my dearest wish for you to become my wife," Jacques announced.

"And all my dreams come true, to have you as my husband," she gushed, almost unable now to contain her joy.

When they went downstairs, they saw that electricians and joiners were working there. They laughed to each other, wondering if they had heard their earlier lovemaking. Her rosy cheeks were enough to convince the workers that something had been going on in the room above their heads, but nobody said anything.

'What a wonderful day this has been,' she thought. The workmen looked at her and smiled as she laughed out loud.

CHAPTER 13
LOVE IS ALL AROUND

It was the day they'd all been working towards. Kali had spent the previous night with Poppy, so she could help her to get ready for the big day. The two of them were chatting until quite late, each telling their own story of how they'd met the men in their lives, although with Poppy having to leave out all the details of her work relationship with Babis. They told how they fell in love, and how they knew that their respective partners were the ones for them.

Kali knew it must be hard and emotional for Poppy not to have her mother and father there to help her, and also not having a father to give her away. A work colleague was to be best man for Babis, and Kali was to be the only bridesmaid or maid of honour.

Kali had related the story of when Babis first came to stay with them, and the long process of his adoption. She told of how he'd been a good brother, well-liked by all, but still scorned by some of the villagers she knew. Babis adored Poppy, and likewise, she adored him.

Kali and Poppy shared anecdotes from their childhood days, along with their expectations for the future. It was getting quite late when they finally retired, setting alarms for early rising, still having lots to do before the ceremony.

The next morning, Kali was awake before Poppy and took her an early morning cup of tea. Poppy was feeling very nervous, so Kali tried to reassure her that all would be fine.

"The best way to relax is to go for a walk along the beach," she advised Poppy. "Come on, we have plenty of time."

The two girls set off arm in arm down the road leading to the beach, walking past Corner Cafe and over the wooden bridge near Syrtaki. They were alone, with no other people to be seen. They took off their shoes and walked along in the soft sand, passing Rainbow and on past Royal Bay. They let the cold sea touch their toes, laughing and smiling at each other.

Soon it was time to walk back, and they both felt a little more relaxed. Now it was showers, hair and makeup, and then finally putting on their beautiful dresses. Poppy had chosen an Empire Line, off white dress, with tiny pearls randomly stitched on the fabric. It was stunning in its simplicity. She wore a hair band that was embroidered with the same tiny pearls.

Kali's dress was aqua blue and in a similar design. She had curled her long dark hair and wore it loose behind a broad headband.

They both stood together in front of the mirror, clutching their bouquets.

"What do we look like, posing like this?" Poppy said, smiling. They both broke out into fits of giggles.

There was a knock on the front door and they tried to compose themselves, this would be the family come to walk the bride to the church in traditional Greek fashion.

Just for a second, Poppy felt sad that her mother and father would not be here on her special day, but then thought of the wonderful family she would very soon be a be part of, and there were so many of them.

Slowly they climbed the incline from the house where Mia and Sophia had begun their married life together, and walked the short distance to the church. Onlookers lined the street and many of the villagers were outside the church hoping to catch a glimpse of the bride. Babis was waiting by the door until the procession turned the corner by Kos Island studios. His best man then led him inside, where the priest was waiting to carry out the marriage ceremony.

A cousin of Babis took Poppy's arm and escorted her into the church. There was much chanting during the service, with Poppy trying her best to interpret what was being said. At the end of the ceremony came the switching of head dresses, followed by the first walk together as man and wife. This completed the ceremony and both she and Babis heaved a sigh of relief.

Now came the time for celebrations. They made the short walk down the road to Ficus restaurant, where Tilly had been so busy decorating the place and setting out the seating so that all the guests had a great view of the bride and groom. The tables had macramé crocheted mats, and rose petals were scattered everywhere. There were dream catchers and beautiful dried flower wreaths, with tiny LED lights entwined with flowers and vine leaves. It was so beautiful.

After the meal and speeches were made, both in Greek and English, came the cutting of the cake, which had been made by another of Mia's friends. Then it was the ideal time for lots of dancing and shouts of 'OPA.'

As the event was coming to a close, with Babis and Poppy about to leave, Mia and Sophia stood together, each clutching a piece of paper. People were shushed by others and silence reigned, as Sophia began to speak.

"Today we have seen our son married to the woman of his dreams, and we have witnessed how happy he is. Most of you know we adopted Babis several years ago as a tiny baby, abandoned by his mother. He has brought us much happiness along with the odd bit of struggle, but we are so very proud of him."

"Today on this happy occasion," Mia began, now taking the floor along with the microphone, "we have received some information that I know not only makes the occasion complete, but has also helped make a dream come true for Babis."

The audience were confused as they listened to Mia, however, clarity was offered when Mia announced. "Please raise your glasses to our new son, Sam, whose adoption papers were completed today."

Babis later led Poppy outside to the waiting car, which would take them to their unknown honeymoon destination. What a wonderful way it was to end this day of celebrations. Now it was time to organise the next.

Jacques had asked Kali to trust him and her mothers with making all the arrangements. He promised not to let her down or disappoint her. At first she was hesitant about handing everything over to Jacques. She had watched the programme on television called, "Don't Tell the Bride," when the groom had done all the arrangements, but quite often it had been a disaster! It was strange for a man to want to arrange a wedding.

"But you don't know people here," Kali protested.

"But your mothers do," Jacques argued.

They had agreed that her wedding dress and those of her bridesmaids were for her to choose, as well as the type of flowers for her bouquet. The rest he would arrange.

On a few occasions, she would ask Jacques about what he had planned, but he would always tell her nothing. Kali knew he had been speaking to her mothers' cousin, Demetris, and to Andreas, but she couldn't get any information from them either.

"What about the guest list?" she asked Jacques.

"Sorted," he told her, nonchalantly.

"And the venue?" she questioned.

"Sorted," he replied.

"What about the transport?" Kali queried.

"Sorted," he said again, and this was the only answer Jacques would give her.

He knew she was frustrated by not knowing but he wanted the perfect day for her and was really working hard to make sure it was just that – her perfect day.

Kali kept herself busy finishing off the decoration of the house and supervising the laying out of the gardens. She had always been told about her great grandmother, Jenny, and how she loved her gardens, even as a young child. As she planned the gardens here at the house now, she imagined her grandma doing the same for her house at the top of the village where she'd been brought up. She recalled the lovely minimalistic gardens surrounding the house and overlooking the cove, where her grandmother had lived for a while. Jenny had told her that planning and planting a garden was having faith in the future, and this here was her future. She was proud of what she'd already achieved.

As the date of the wedding drew nearer, Jacques became more and more secretive, with Kali becoming more and more nervous because of it, although she knew she needed to trust Jacques and her mothers.

Of course there had been the traditional mother and daughter trip to Athens to buy outfits for Sophia and Mia, along with, of course, her own wedding dress.

The dress Kali chose was just like the dress she had once seen in an historical drama. It was ivory in colour, with short puff sleeves and a wide low neck, fitted tightly under the bust and then falling loosely to the floor. It was made of silk and covered with fine French lace, with a short train at the back. This dress was her tribute to Jacques, and she complemented it with a wide head dress with a crocheted flower on one side.

Both mothers were delighted with her choice. Mia chose a pale blue dress and a short jacket, whilst Sophia chose a pale lemon dress and long jacket. Kali was so proud of them when she saw them trying on their choices.

It had been decided that Babis would take the father's role of giving Kali away, and that Sam would be one of the groomsmen. Kali's school pal and best friend would stand for her as maid of honour, and her friend's two little daughters would be bridesmaids.

Jacques' mother and her sister would be flying in from France to attend the wedding, and Jacques and Kali were to collect them from the airport. Kali was a little nervous at meeting his mother, as he'd told her very little about his future wife. She wondered if all the mothers' would get on together, and also how she would be as Kali's mother in law.

Jacques' father had passed away some time ago and his mother had moved in with her younger sister. As Jacques' mother's health had deteriorated, her sister had become a carer for her.

Jacques had been concerned that the travel to Kos might be too exhausting for her, but she had told him in no uncertain terms that she was most definitely coming.

As well as Kali, Jacques also seemed a little nervous as they headed to the airport. They waited in arrivals for the two women to come through the sliding doors from baggage reclaim, but then Jacques spotted them. His Aunt was steering the wheelchair, whilst an airport attendant carefully juggled with the luggage on a trolley.

When Kali saw them, she could see that Jacques' mother had once been a stunningly beautiful woman. She had an air of aristocracy about her, and the two sisters reminded her of the English Queen and her younger sister, Princess Margaret. They were very stylishly dressed, considering they were travelling.

Jacques went forward to greet them, leaning down to kiss his mother in the wheelchair. She held up her hand to touch Jacques' face in a show of affection. Kali waited until Jacques had also greeted his Aunt, then he turned to her and beckoned her to come and meet them. Kali spoke in her best French accent.

"Bienvenue Madam," she said, feeling like she should curtsy, in deference to her apparent status.

"Merci. Vous parlez Francais?" Jacques' mother replied, eyeing Kali up and down.

"Mais oui," Kali replied.

Jacques mother turned to Jacques. "Elle est tres jolie," she told him. Jacques thought this was quite an approval – Praise indeed.

Once they were all in the car and the wheelchair and luggage had been loaded, they began their journey to Kefalos. Jacques began to tell them a little of the history of the island and how it had been invaded in the past by the Turks, Italians and The Germans. He began pointing out various places of interest along the route.

"To the right was the road to Plaka, where you could visit the peacocks. On the left was the volcanic island of Nisyros, and later on the right is the island of Kalymnos," he instructed.

He then told them of his now favourite beach, Volcania. He went on to explain that this was the narrowest part of the island, and you could see the sea at both sides. He told them, as they neared Kamari, to look at the picturesque tiny island of Kastri, out in the bay.

All his explanations had been in French, but Kali had managed to understand most of what he'd said. However, this far there had been no response from the ladies seated in the back of the car. During the journey, Kali had felt like there were eyes piercing into the back of her head, and she felt a little uncomfortable about this.

The ladies were staying at Ikos, so Jacques pulled up outside the security point and spoke to the guards, who lifted the barrier so that he could drive inside. They had rented a villa with a pool to give them privacy.

As they walked from the car and moved towards the villa, Kali felt a hand grab hold of her arm. It was Jacques' mother. She spoke in perfect English, as she addressed Kali.

"Do you love my son?" she interrogated. Before Kali had chance to reply, Jacques' mother spoke again. "He is a good boy and I do not want him to get hurt again," she said sharply. Kali was about to reply when she was interrupted again.

"Does your family have money?" Kali thought this was very rude and inappropriate. She paused before she replied.

"To answer your first question, Yes, I love Jacques very much." Kali wanted to add that some of her family were actually millionaires, but she didn't. "I knew from the moment I met him that he was a wonderful man," she did however say.

"And can you have children?" his mother questioned. Kali was shocked by the bluntness of the question, but listened as she said, "I want my son to have children, more than one, not like me."

Jacques aunt looked embarrassed at the level, and tone, of the questioning. Kali carefully worded her reply.

"I have never thought of the possibility that I could not have children, so I suppose, yes, I think that there is a strong chance I could. I would love to have children and I know Jacques would make a wonderful father. I am so happy to be marrying Jacques, and I hope you can also be happy for us too."

Jacques mother thought about it for a second or two and then said, "I am happy. I can see how much my son means to you." She said this with such sincerity that Kali was taken aback, given how harshly she'd just been interrogated.

His mother then leant forward in her wheelchair and held out her arm to embrace Kali. 'What a change in her attitude,' Kali thought.

Jacques had been watching all this and heaved a sigh of relief. His mother could be quite cantankerous at times, but he could tell by her actions that she had accepted Kali.

Jacques and Kali made sure the ladies had everything they needed and then left, saying they would return in the morning to check everything was okay, and also to let them know the arrangements for the day of the wedding.

"So far so good," Jacques muttered, as they drove back to Kefalos village. He looked far more relaxed now, and so did Kali. What an ordeal for them both. Fingers crossed that everything else would go smoothly.

It was now only days away. Kali still had no idea of where the wedding would be taking place, or who would be there. In fact, she knew nothing at all.

She was feeling a little sick this morning and hoped she wasn't going to be ill, just before the wedding. She put it down to nerves and stress. After all, it was a stressful occasion.

When the day of the wedding finally dawned, Mia and Sophia fussed over their daughter, instructing the hairdresser just how her hair should be best styled. The makeup artist raised her eyes to the ceiling more than once when the mothers' couldn't agree what shade of eye shadow Kali should have.

Kali was feeling quite relaxed whilst sitting in front of the mirror in her white bathrobe, but then she suddenly stood up and ran to the bathroom, where she was violently sick!

"It's just nerves," Sophia told her. "Here, eat this plain biscuit. It will settle your stomach." Kali did as she was told and soon felt okay again.

It was almost time to leave and Kali only needed to put on her dress, all the time watched by her two mums, who were already dressed and waiting for their daughter. As ever, it was an emotional moment for a mother to see her daughter in a wedding dress, and today it was emotional times two! The three of them hugged, the last time they would, with Kali still being a single woman.

When someone knocked at the door, they knew it was time for them to leave. They let Babis takeover, but he seemed even more nervous than Kali. He walked her down the steps at the front of the house, where a beautiful flower covered horse and carriage awaited, driven expertly by Damon and Maisie's son, Alexander.

"Where are we going?" Kali asked Babis.

"You'll see." he said smiling.

Alexander carefully steered the horse and carriage down the steep road leading to the harbour. He pulled the reigns and the horse came to a stop at the extreme end of it. The little boat that was always used to ferry brides to their wedding at the little church on the island was moored there, patiently awaiting the arrival of the latest bride - Kali.

She tried her best not to cry when she remembered that this was the exact spot where her great grandmother, Jenny, had been married to her second husband, Yiannis, many years before.

"I guess I'm getting married on the island then," she said to Babis.

"You'll see," Babis replied, as he helped her board the little boat and then sat beside her. She reached out to hold his hand, as nerves were now getting the better of her.

Kali was surprised when the boat didn't head for the island, but went in the opposite direction around the headland. She thought it could be the little secluded beach, where Laura and Nikos had been married, but as they rounded the headland, there, anchored in the sea just off the coast was a marvellous looking, gigantic super yacht. The shock of seeing this made her gasp for air. Their little boat headed towards it and Kali could see that it was full of people. She looked at Babis, confused.

"You'll see," she mimicked. "Is that all you can say?"

"Just trust Jacques," he replied, whilst laughing at her.

"How will we get aboard?" she asked. Babis turned to her, but before he could say anything, she answered for him. "I know - you'll see," she exclaimed.

Two metal doors on the side of the yacht opened and a platform was extended. With Babis' helping hand, and that of a crew member, Kali stepped aboard and was escorted up the metal staircase and onto the deck.

Cheers immediately went up from the crowd already waiting onboard. Some of them she knew, some of them she wasn't sure whether she knew them or not, but some she certainly didn't know at all. She could see Jacques' mother prominently positioned like a member of the royal family, and this made her smile.

A plush carpet lay across the deck, leading up to a beautiful wrought iron arbour covered in beautiful and variously coloured roses. A celebrant stood in the centre, and at the side stood Jacques and his best man. He looked fabulous in a beige suit and white shirt, almost the same colour as Kali's dress. He turned and smiled at her. She waved a finger at him and then smiled back.

The ceremony was very moving and said in three languages, Greek, French and English. When they were pronounced man and wife, the applause of the congregation was incredible. They went inside where everything was arranged for fine dining, and then through the double doors into a very large dance area. It all went like clockwork. Jacques had thought of every little detail. How could she not love him?

"How did you manage to hire the yacht?" she asked him a little later.

"I remembered that a very influential associate of mine told me about a yacht he'd commissioned to be built by a firm in Athens, and that the family who owned the firm came from Kefalos. I spoke to Nikos and Demetris and they gave me the location of the yacht. It was by a miracle, in Greek waters. My associate, who always liked to show off, agreed to sail to Kos and allow us to have the wedding on board.

Perhaps you should thank him, Kali. He's standing over there in the blue suit with the young girl. I am sure he would be delighted to meet you and tell you all about the yacht. That is if you have about twelve hours to spare."

"I might catch him later," Kali said. "I don't want to leave my husband's side, not even for one minute today."

It was just over a month since Jacques and Kali had been married. They had now moved permanently into the house on the far outskirts of the village. Although there was still work outstanding to be completed in the interior of the house, they had plenty of time to do this.

Kali continued to work at the office as well as from home. She worked non-stop, and Jacques frequently told her to slow down.

They relaxed in each other's arms every evening, quite content to sit without conversation, just savouring the closeness they felt in each other's company.

Kali had complained that she was tired a couple of times, but she'd been very busy. Tonight though, she fell asleep in Jacques' arms. He carried her to their bedroom and laid her on the bed. Covering her with a blanket, he let her sleep. When she awoke the next morning, she had no recollection of being carried to bed.

"Perhaps you are just a little exhausted," he suggested. "Maybe you need a tonic, or something."

"Maybe, but I could be slightly anaemic. I'll get it checked out at the doctor," she told her husband.

"Good idea," he agreed.

A couple of days later, she was feeling a little light headed, so decided to call in to see the local doctor. She was lucky as there was no one waiting, so she went straight in. The doctor was surprised to see her, as she was one of his least frequent visitors.

"I'm feeling a little tired and light headed, Doctor," she explained.

The doctor examined her, but finding nothing obvious, he suggested a couple of tests be done. Kali began to feel a little silly about such a fuss being made, especially if there was nothing wrong with her.

Later that week, when she received a phone call at the office asking her to return to the surgery, she began to panic as to what the tests could have revealed.

She nervously sat in the waiting room. This time she was not so lucky and it seemed there were quite a few people in the queue ahead of her. When the door to the consulting room opened, the doctor came out to talk to the receptionist with the patient he'd just seen. He looked across and saw Kali waiting patiently, so motioned for her to go into the consulting room, although there were a few 'tuts' from the other people also waiting to see the doctor.

"Take a seat, Kali," said the doctor, sitting down behind his desk and placing his hands upon it. "Well, I have the results of the tests we did earlier in the week." Kali took a large intake of breath, as the doctor continued. "Now I have some news for you, and I hope it won't come as a shock."

"Oh my god, what is wrong with me?" she pleaded.

"Nothing, nothing at all," he revealed. Kali looked at him, needing an explanation. "My dear, you are going to have a baby. You're pregnant," he announced.

"A baby, when?" she asked, not believing what she was hearing.

"Well that is what we now need to find out," Doctor Galanis motioned. "I want you to go for a scan at the medical centre, and then we can check things out." Kali nodded, but was completely lost for words. "Don't worry my dear. I can

155

ring now if you like, and I can make an appointment for you," Doctor Galanis suggested.

"Okay, thank you, but I think I'd better tell my husband," Kali said, trembling and trying to take in the news.

The doctor arranged a scan for two days' time and Kali went home in a daze. When she arrived, Jacques was already at home, so she had little time to prepare what to say to him.

"I have been to the doctors," she began, a little flustered. "I have to have a scan." Jacques looked so worried. "Don't worry, I'm only having a baby," she blurted.

"What!" Jacques shouted in shock at the announcement. "You're pregnant?"

"I'm sorry, I didn't know," she said, now feeling really guilty.

"Tell me again," Jacques said to her.

"I'm sorry, I'm having a baby," she repeated.

"You're sorry! Why are you sorry? Are you not happy?" he questioned, looking very concerned.

"Of course I'm happy, but it was a shock. I never thought I might be pregnant," Kali stated.

"You're pregnant. This is wonderful news," Jacques said with the biggest smile on his face. "When is the baby due?"

"That's why I am having the scan. The doctor can't be sure," she confirmed.

"You fill my life with such happiness," Jacques said with great emotion, as he threw his arms around Kali.

A few days later, they went together for the scan. Jacques was very quiet during the preliminary part of the examination. The screen was turned away from them and they were anxious for an answer about the baby. The doctor kept repeating the scan, all the time looking intently at the screen.

"Is there something wrong?" asked Jacques, trying to lean forward to look at the screen.

"No, not really," the doctor said.

Jacques jumped up from his chair. "What do you mean, not really?" he demanded.

"Calm down, Sir," the doctor said, trying to reassure Jacques that nothing was amiss.

"Is the baby okay?" Kali queried, looking very close to tears.

"The baby?" the doctor asked, looking confused.

"Yes, the baby," Jacques and Kali both said together.

"Oh, yes the baby is okay, and so is the other one!" the doctor exclaimed.

"The other one," Jacques asked, needing clarity. At the same time, Kali nearly fainted.

"You two are carrying twins," the doctor announced. "Two bouncing babies, not one, and looking at the size of them, you are probably about three months pregnant.

"Not quite a honeymoon baby, or babies then," Kali said, looking shyly at Jacques.

The doctor assured them that everything was fine, and appointments would be made for antenatal care.

"Congratulations," the doctor said. "I am very happy for you both." Kali and Jacques left the surgery, shocked, but extremely happy.

By the time Kali had reached four months of pregnancy, she was filling out and felt people were going to be noticing, as she had always been a trim girl. It was time to tell the family.

Jacques telephoned his mother to tell her the news. She was pleased for them but told Jacques rather bluntly, "I thought she would be a good breeder." 'His mother always did have a good way with words,' he thought.

As always, a family gathering was organised and everyone who could, came to Jacques' and Kali's house. There were chairs laid out on the rear patio, and tables covered with snacks and mezes.

"Everyone quiet please," Jacques requested, asking for his attention to be noted, which was hard to get with so many Greeks gathered together. Kali stood by his side as he began the announcement.

"My wife and I….." Jacques began, and there was a cheer from the family. "My wife and I," he continued, "would like to make an announcement. We have had some wonderful news and would like to share our happiness with you. We want to tell you that we are expecting……"

Before Jacques could finish, a roar went up from the family. Having children was so important, and this was the first announcement of the next generation.

"I'll try again," he smiled, as the noise subsided. "I want to tell you that we are expecting twins, yes, twins! Kali and I both feel as though we have been truly blessed."

As Kali heard these words being said by Jacques, she remembered what the old lady at the gipsy camp had told her that day when she'd read her Tarot cards.

It had all come true. She had found Jacques, a man who was not from these shores and he had helped her with her task. He had stolen her heart, and now, even more importantly, had given her the two blessings which the woman had mentioned. How could she have known? Kali smiled, patting her ever growing stomach affectionately.

"Yes, my little blessings," Kali whispered, "stay tucked in there until the time is right, and I guess some starry night you will come into this world."

Babis came across to Kali to congratulate her, and also whispered something in her ear.

"No," she shrieked with laughter and with a smile all over her face. "That's wonderful."

Kali held up her hand and shushed the gathering. "My brother also has an announcement to make. Over to you, brother." Babis looked very emotional as he began to speak.

"Poppy is not with us today, she had an appointment elsewhere, but she gave me permission to tell you that we too are thrilled to announce we are expecting.

I know Kali, my big sister always has to go one better than me," he laughed. "We are expecting just the one, but we're equally delighted about our little one." He finished off by saying, "What a truly fantastic day this is for all the family."

There were cheers and whistles all round, and everyone came forward to hug Jacques, Kali and Babis.

"Well, Sam, you are going to be a very busy uncle," Kali joked with her newly adopted brother.

Happily, new Uncle Sam loved his new family, and today he was bursting with pride.

CHAPTER 14
TOULA AND DEMETRIS

Laura's two children, Demetris and Toula, continued to live in their homes in the village. Demetris ran the yacht building company and Toula continued to practice medicine at the centre.

It was well known in the village that the family were very influential and their father, Nikos, had provided funds for various improvements, including the building of the paediatric centre.

None of the family ever bragged about money, all being actively involved in charity and community work.

They loved living in Kefalos and were happy, and content, with their lives there. However, there came a time when all the happiness and contentment of the entire family was ripped to shreds.

Toula would walk down to the beach at Cavos for an early morning swim before starting work. She loved the quiet time before the tourist world woke. She'd always done this for months and months at the same time each day, spending the same amount of time in the water, leaving at the same time, and allowing her the time to shower and get ready for work.

She didn't take much notice of what was going on around her during this routine, until one morning when she spotted a black van parked near the harbour steps. At first, she thought it was one of the transfer vehicles with its blacked-out windows. She didn't give it a second thought, but when it was there again on the next day, she began to wonder what it was doing here at such an early time of the day. She had a funny sensation that she was being watched, although she shook her head and dismissed the thought and continued to go to the beach each day. Sometimes the van was there, other times it was not. She eventually lost interest, but sometimes still felt like she was being watched.

This particular morning, Toula took her swim, dried herself, and climbed the steps from the beach. As she passed the van, the rear doors opened and a man jumped out and startled her. He threw something over her head and bundled her into the back of the van. He pressed a pungent smelling cloth over her nostrils and everything went black.

As Toula lived alone, no one would notice that she hadn't returned home. It was when she hadn't arrived at work that her colleagues wondered where she was. She was always the first to arrive each day and was normally so punctual.

They rang her home to find out if she was ill, but they received no reply. Perhaps she was on her way, but when she didn't arrive they contacted Laura, who said she would check at the house.

When Laura went to the house, the gates were locked and there was no sign of her. This all felt very wrong and she immediately suspected that something bad had happened to Toula so she alerted the family, who also tried to find her. This was so out of character for Toula.

Mia and Sophia had deep empathy for Toula's parents, having had the heartache of the disappearance of their son, Babis. Demetris suggested they spoke to the police, whilst he went down to the harbour and asked around there.

It was now several hours since they'd discovered she was missing and panic had now began to set in.

The police arrived and questioned all the family members. They knew the family well, and many of the officers had grown up with Toula. They wished Babis was there with them, but he was in Athens at a police conference, however, as soon as he found out about her disappearance, he caught the first plane back and was ready to take over the investigation.

They searched everywhere and asked everyone they knew, just in case someone had seen her, but no one came forward.

Laura and Nikos thought about offering a reward to anyone who could help them find their daughter. Members of the family took it in turns to stay with Laura, whilst Nikos spent time speaking to people and searching the places she would normally frequent.

It was a few days later when Nikos received a telephone call. A muffled voice was heard, telling him that they had Toula.

"I promise no harm will come to her as long as you pay the ransom," the muffled voice was heard to say.

"How much is the ransom?" Nikos asked, trying desperately to control his feelings.

"I want you to pay one million euros," the kidnapper demanded. "Pay this and I guarantee her safe return. He went on to say that if this sum was not paid quickly, they couldn't guarantee her safety, or what might happen to her.

Nikos was speechless! His hands were shaking, as emotion and dread surged through his body. He really didn't know what to do next.

Babis came to speak with Nikos, whilst his crew fitted devices to the phone in readiness for any communication from the kidnappers, but they heard nothing.

Kali thought she knew someone who could help them. She remembered how accurate the gipsy woman had been when predicting her own future. As well as hoping that the woman could provide some help in the search for Toula, Kali also wanted to thank her, and so she took herself off back to the gipsy camp.

She walked a little unsteadily along the gravel path leading to the camp. When she arrived at the destination, she saw sitting there before her was the woman, just like last time, sat in a chair outside her caravan. She looked up as Kali approached, and Kali could tell that she recognised her. The old woman grimaced.

"I told you never to return," the woman said sternly. "I said I could not help you and not to come back."

"But I came back to thank you for what you told me that time. It has all since come true," Kali informed the woman. "However, I now need to ask for your help in another matter, a very serious matter!" As Kali said this, she took out a fifty euro note to give to the woman, at which the old woman looked intrigued.

"It must be important for you to return here against my instructions," she said through gapped teeth. "Come and sit down. Tell me about you first."

Kali told her how she'd met Jacques and how he had helped in her task. How she'd fallen in love with him, and that, quite recently, they'd been married. The old woman first looked at Kali's stomach, and then into her eyes.

"You have had your two blessings, the blessings which I predicted, haven't you," asked the woman, whilst pointing at Kali's stomach. Kali nodded, gently stroking her growing lump.

"Your life will be truly blessed," the woman revealed. "Now, why do you search again? Who is lost?" she questioned.

Kali sat beside the woman and began to relate how Toula had gone missing. "We believe that she's been kidnapped," Kali stated. The old gipsy closed her eyes.

"She is with someone who is known to a family member," the gipsy woman articulated. "He keeps her in the dark and she cannot move."

Kali was shaken by this and wanted to cry as the woman continued. "All I will say to you is; tell the tall dark man who you searched for before, to go to the church." Kali felt a little confused as she continued to listen. "I cannot give you any more about this. You must tell the man to go to the church," the woman told her.

"Thank you," Kali said, although wondering if she had just parted with fifty euros for nothing, but then, the woman spoke again.

"Your children will make you proud. You will be a good mother and the man who gave them to you will never stray from your side." She looked at Kali and half smiled. "Go now. Tell the man what I have told you."

"Can I ask you one more question?" Kali ventured to ask. The old woman looked directly at Kali as she asked. "Was it you?"

"Was it me who took the child to the clinic in Kefalos that day? Is this the question you are asking me?"

"Yes it is," Kali replied. The woman looked thoughtful for a moment, but then replied to the question.

Yes, my dear, it was me. I did it so the child would have a better life than the one the mother could ever provide."

"Thank you for being so honest," Kali told the old gipsy woman, who smiled at her.

"Your brother is a good man," she replied, dismissing Kali by standing and walking up the steps and into her caravan. She then closed the door on Kali, perhaps forever.

Kali was quite exhausted when she arrived back at her home. She asked Jacques to take her to see Babis.

When they arrived, Babis was not sure what to make of the message from the gipsy, but Kali was so insistent that she'd been very accurate regarding events in her own life, that Babis stored the information in his head. If it became relevant for any reason, he would heed it.

When the call came for Nikos, Babis told him to wait a little time before picking up the phone, "So the equipment can do its work and hopefully trace the call," he instructed. When the call came, Babis nodded to Nikos and he gingerly picked up the phone.

"Kalimera," he said in Greek.

"English," the muffled voice replied.

"Okay, English," Nikos managed to say.

"No Police or all deals are off," the voice demanded.

"Okay," Nikos lied, with his nephew standing beside him and listening to everything.

"What do you want me to do?" Nikos questioned.

"Do you have the cash?" the voice asked.

"Not until tomorrow. The bank couldn't do it," Nikos told the caller.

"That's not good," the caller said, sounding angry.

Nikos looked pleadingly at Babis. "I will have it tomorrow," he whispered to Babis. At that moment, the line went dead.

"What do we do now?" asked Nikos, looking thoroughly shattered.

"We wait," Babis told him. "It's all we can do."

Another day passed and Laura and Nikos were falling apart with worry for the daughter they loved so very much. It was almost twelve o'clock noon, but still no phone call. But at one-thirty, the phone finally rang.

Babis signalled to Nikos, slowly, slowly, slowly, until Nikos picked up the phone.

"Yes," he said.

"Do you have it?" the kidnapper said gruffly. "Do you have the money?"

"Yes, I do," Nikos told him.

"Go alone to Agios Theologos," the voice began. "I will be watching. Go now," the line went dead, leaving very little time for anything to be traced or organised.

Toula had absolutely no idea where she was. It smelt musty and damp, and also felt cold. All she could do was listen, as she had been blindfolded and gagged so she couldn't call out. She thought she might be in some sort of animal shelter.

The kidnapper had told her there was a toilet, but it wasn't connected to the water supply. She was made to ask if she wanted to use it.

"I will return in the morning," the kidnapper informed her as he was about to leave. She felt terrified being in the pitch-black and listening to every strange sound in the night.

Toula felt like she could hear the sea, but it seemed to be way below her. She could hear traffic in the distance but even if she was able to call out, it was much too far away for her to be heard.

She barely slept and had no concept of time, but suddenly there was the sound of rocks falling. She wondered if it was morning and the kidnapper was returning. Sadly, her assumption was true.

"I have brought some food for you, and something to drink," the gruff voice told her. "I will remove the gag from you if you promise not to scream. Do you promise?"

"Yes, I promise," Toula surrendered.

"Good," the voice said. "Although it wouldn't matter, as nobody will hear you," he laughed.

He removed the gag and put some food into her hand. She was told it was a croissant. It was difficult for Toula to eat, as her hands remained tied together with ropes that dug into her wrists and ankles.

Having eaten the croissant, he offered her a bottle of water which she struggled to open. He grabbed it from her, opened it, and pushed it back in her hands. The water was warm but Toula welcomed it, as her lips were parched and sore.

"Why are you doing this to me?" she cried.

"Shut up!" he demanded, and that was the end of that conversation!

Toula tried to remain calm, but each time she heard movement, she flinched. She had no idea what he might do to her.

The routine was much the same for the next few days, croissant and water in the morning, then left alone all day to fend for herself until what she believed was night fall, when he brought her scraps of meat and bread, or a cheese pie. He hardly spoke and never stayed long when he visited.

Toula despaired of ever getting away and wondered what the kidnapper might do if any ransom demand wasn't paid. Perhaps he would abandon her, leave her here to die alone, or even kill her in his desperation.

She prayed with all her heart for release from this dreadful situation, and then one day, maybe her prayers were answered. One morning he didn't bring her breakfast, but came later.

"Get up," he demanded. "You're coming with me."

'Maybe my prayers HAVE been answered,' she thought hopefully.

The kidnapper made sure the gag was in place and the blindfold had been securely fastened, and he checked that the ropes were snugly fitted to her wrists. He half walked and half carried her as they scrambled uphill, all the time scratching her hands and knees, which she was sure were now bleeding.

Again she listened as best she could. The traffic seemed louder than it had previously. She heard a car door open and was pushed inside.

The journey wasn't a long one, but again, when she was pulled out of the car she had no idea where she was. The air tasted salty, and she thought it might be sand under her feet.

The kidnapper helped her up a couple of steps and Toula heard him unlock a door. He then pushed her inside, before locking the door behind him and leaving. She stumbled and fell to the floor. There in the pitch black, she remained flat on her face. She cried bitterly with emotion.

"Will this nightmare never end?" she cried.

She heard the car drive off. Her stomach rumbled and her lips were sore from wearing the gag, but the next thing she heard was the door being unlocked and opened. She felt strong arms turn her over onto her back, and then a soft and gentle voice spoke to her.

"Lie still and be quiet," a voice said. "I will come back for you." Toula was confused as it didn't sound like her kidnapper. She did as she was told and stayed still. From sheer lack of food and exhaustion, she soon fell asleep.

Nikos looked at Babis for his advice. Babis went into the next room and made a few quick phone calls from his mobile and then returned to the room.

"Go slowly and calmly," he said, turning to Nikos. "Don't do anything heroic that might jeopardise things, or cause the kidnapper to act irrationally."

Nikos was trembling as he left the house and set off in his car. He knew there was a tracking device in the moneybag he carried, but was afraid the kidnapper might also discover it. He drove as slowly as his nerves would allow down the long and winding road that led to Agios Theologos. As he passed all the little churches on the way, he crossed himself and asked God to protect his daughter, Toula.

He parked close to the restaurant, which was closed for the winter and waited for what seemed like an eternity, before a battered old silver car slowed down to a stop. The driver, who wore a scarf around his face, looked directly at Nikos and gestured for him to follow. With his nerves really on edge by now, Nikos had no choice but to follow.

He drove down the sandy, rutted track that led along the edge of the cliffs which sloped down into the sea. The silver car stopped near the little church and Nikos pulled up close to it. He waited to see if the driver would get out and come to him, or whether he was supposed to deliver the bag to the waiting car.

Eventually the man beckoned to Nikos to come to the car. Nikos slowly eased himself out of his car, at the same time retrieving the bag from the back seat. The man opened the back door of the car as Nikos arrived.

"Don't turn around," he ordered, and then told Nikos to put the bag on the back seat. As Nikos placed the bag down, the man pulled out a knife. He looked very nervous and Nikos didn't want to do anything to antagonise him.

"Get out now and stand next to the car," the man shouted. Nikos did as was ordered, with beads of sweat now running down his cheeks. The man opened the bag and looked inside. He saw the notes were carefully packed in plastic bags and allowed himself a smile.

As he was turning to get out of the car, he caught his scarf on the seatbelt and it fell down, revealing his face. Now the stakes had changed, as Nikos knew what he looked like. The kidnapper panicked and lunged towards Nikos with the knife, but he managed to side-step the blade and avoided the thrust.

At that moment the door of the little church opened and out stepped a priest in his flowing black robes. The attacker, who Nikos now knew was the kidnapper, pulled him in front of him and held the knife in his back.

"Keep still and keep your mouth shut," he ordered Nikos, as the priest walked towards them. "It's okay father," the kidnapper said. "He's had too much ouzo."

"Well my son, let me help you," the priest suggested.

"No, no it's okay" the man said, now starting to panic.

The priest walked right up to them and pulled Nikos from the kidnappers grip. As he did this, he was faced with the frightened man with a knife, who just wanted to escape with the money. He lunged towards the priest, but the holy man grabbed his wrist.

All Nikos could do was watch in amazement as the priest wrestled with the man, who finally dropped the knife. He turned and ran to the car and drove off.

"Are you okay my son?" he priest asked, turning to Nikos. He then began laughing hysterically.

Confused by what had just happened, Nikos looked at the priest, who was now tugging at his beard. He watched as the beard came off in his hands. The priest then removed the hat and veil and Nikos was now stunned! For standing there, disrobed before him was none other than Babis.

"He has gone, but we don't know where Toula is," Nikos said, now furious with Babis. "She might even be dead and it's your fault." Hearing Nikos saying this, all Babis could do was smile.

"So, you think it's funny, do you?" Nikos demanded through clenched teeth.

"Come Nikos, you need some spiritual help," Babis said calmly. "Just come into the church with me."

"Don't be such a fool Babis," Nikos retorted.

Babis grabbed his arm and gently pushed him towards the little church. He opened the door and there bound and gagged was Toula. Nikos could barely believe his eyes.

They carefully took off the ropes and tape. Toula burst into tears but they were tears of relief. Nikos hugged her so hard it almost took her breath away.

"What now?" Nikos asked, turning to Babis.

"Your money is safe," he explained to Nikos.

"I don't care about the money," Nikos said. "I want to know what the hell just happened."

"Nikos, you have your daughter back and she is unharmed," Babis expressed. "You should be happy, not angry."

"I'm not angry, Babis," Nikos confirmed much calmer now. "But how did this happen?"

"Someone told me to go to the little church," Babis revealed. Nikos looked at Babis as if he was crazy, but listened as he continued to explain. "It was all too amateurish, not like a professional kidnap. More like in the movies, or even a video game.

There are several ways to get down here that not many people are aware of, or even if they are, most will not have a vehicle that can drive down these roads.

I arranged roadblocks on all the exits, once the suspect's car had passed. There wasn't anywhere else to hide anyone here, and I didn't think the kidnapper would want to leave Toula back where he's been holding her."

Babis stopped as he'd received a call on his mobile. Nikos listened to the one sided conversation and then Babis returned.

"The call I have just received on my mobile told me they caught him red-handed. He is a youth from the village, whom I actually knew from my time as a down and out. I could see he was getting more and more out of control, so that's why I had to act quickly to disarm him when he attacked you.

I knew he had used a knife previously at a shop robbery. I have to admit I was a little frightened at the time, but the rush of adrenaline helped me." As Babis was saying all this, Nikos noticed blood trickling down his arm.

"Have you've been hurt?" Nikos questioned. "Here, let me see."

"It's only a small nick," Babis said, and they both laughed.

"My God, Babis, you are a real star," Nikos claimed. "How can I ever thank you?"

"Come on, Nikos. Let's all go home," Babis suggested. Nikos put his arm round Toula and led her to the car.

Babis jumped in his car, which he'd parked behind the gorse bushes completely out of sight. He followed Nikos and

Toula back to the villa, where police were already waiting to take statements.

Laura had been told that Toula was safe and well. She just couldn't wait to throw her arms around her, just as soon as she arrived home.

Toula told them she had been held in a makeshift hut on the side of the cliff at Marcos beach. The guy had fed her and given her a blanket at night, but nothing more. She'd definitely been traumatised by the entire affair, and because of this, was now being offered counselling.

Nothing like this had ever happened on the island of Kos before, especially not in sleepy Kefalos. The villagers heard the story of his bravery and many now came to congratulate Babis, and of course, to thank him.

He now had what he'd always wanted and been hoping for, he now had the total respect of the villagers. However, he had more than respect, he was now their hero!

Of course, it was cause for a huge celebration, so every family member was invited to the villa for a very happy family gathering.

CHAPTER 15
NEW LOVE FOR TOULA

It took a long time for Toula to recover from the kidnap ordeal, but with the help of a counsellor, along with her loving family, she blossomed and once again became the happy young woman she'd always previously been.

However, she was now more careful and vigilant and varied the time and place for her morning dips, changing her routine frequently, just in case.

One morning, whilst at Kastri beach she was just coming out of the water when she caught sight of a young man paddle boarding along the edge of the sea. She stopped to let him pass, but as he raised his arm to thank her, he lost his balance and fell into the water and Toula couldn't help but laugh. Shaking his hair to rid it of water, he glared at her but then began to laugh himself.

They both walked out of the sea and the young man dragged the paddle board along the sand. He turned to Toula and bravely introduced himself.

"I'm Peter," he said, and smiled in her direction.

"I'm Toula," she returned.

"That's a Greek name, isn't it?" he questioned.

"Yes, my father is Greek, but my mother is English," Toula confirmed.

Peter sat cross legged on the sand. Toula wrapped her towel around her and also sat down next to him. Happily, she did not feel afraid of the young man. Perhaps for the first time since the kidnap, she felt she had a connection with someone.

"Do you live in Kefalos?" she asked.

"No," he answered, but then hesitated.

'What a shame,' Toula thought. 'He's only here on holiday.'

"When I said no, I mean, not yet," Peter went on to say.

"How do you mean, not yet?" Toula enquired.

"My family have bought a house near Limnionis. We will be moving here at the end of the season," he told her.

'That's good,' thought Toula, but wondered if she'd said it out loud.

"I'm here trying to find a job for the summer, but perhaps not trying hard enough," he said with a laugh. "I am enjoying the sea here far too much."

"Why not try the water sports guys. They're frequently looking for staff," Toula suggested.

"I'm actually a qualified gardener," Peter told her.

"Really," Toula said. "Then I may know of someone who needs a gardener."

"You are joking, aren't you?" he smiled.

"Look, I have to go now, or I'll be late for work. Will you be here at the same time tomorrow?" Toula asked, standing up and now ready to leave.

"I can be," he answered.

"Okay, leave it with me. I'll see what I can do," she said whilst turning to go.

"Hey, thanks for that. It was really nice to have met you," Peter told her.

"You too," she shouted over her shoulder as she walked away.

She thought a lot about Peter during the day and remembered to phone her mother with news that she had found her a potential gardener. Laura had been looking for a gardener for a while, as the gardens were too much work for her now that her old gardener had retired.

Sure enough, when Toula went down to Kastri beach the next morning, Peter was sitting on his paddle board staring out to sea. She crept up behind him and gently slapped him on his shoulders, making him jump. He turned around to see who it was and his wide grin showed Toula that he was genuinely pleased to see her.

They chatted for a little while and then Toula suggested they go for a quick dip in the sea. After a relaxing swim, they returned again to conversation.

"Are you able to come with me later to meet someone who wants a gardener?" she asked, not wanting to tell him it was her mum at this stage.

"Well, yes, I have nothing in my diary," he smiled and then laughed. Toula thought he had a lovely smile. It lit up his face and made his eyes shine.

"Do you want to follow me up to the village?" Toula asked, after they'd dried off and dressed quickly.

"How fast do you drive?" he asked her, confusing her slightly.

"Why?" she asked. "Are you not used to driving here?"

"I don't have a car," he confessed. "Not yet anyway, but I could run behind you!"

"Idiot," she exclaimed, beginning to really like this boy. "Okay," she continued. "I'll take you there and drop you off after. I'm not working today, so that'll be fine," Toula told him. They walked to the car park and Toula went to open the door.

"Nice wheels," he said admiringly, when he saw her little Mercedes convertible.

"Thanks," she returned.

Toula drove to the far side of the village, which Peter had not been to before. He seemed glued to the view, looking out of the window at the villas and houses that seemed to get bigger and bigger the further they went.

When Toula pulled up outside of the gates of her parents' villa and pressed the remote control which opened the massive gates, Peter looked overwhelmed.

"Is this your place?" he questioned, feeling absolutely gobsmacked and wondering just who this girl was.

"It's my parents' home, but I did live here before," she replied. Peter was impressed by this, but when he saw the extent of the gardens beyond the gates, he was in heaven.

Laura answered the door. She smiled at her daughter but gave nothing away. Peter tentatively offered his hand to shake Laura's and she broke the ice.

"Toula tells me you are a qualified gardener and you are looking for work. Is that true?" Laura questioned the young man.

"Yes," Peter replied. "I will be moving here with my parents at the end of the season, but if I find work I will stay for the season."

"Are they moving here to Kefalos," Laura asked.

"Yes, near Limnionis," Peter stated.

"How nice, we can see the harbour of Limnionis from the back of our house," Laura informed Peter. "Well then, shall we take a walk in the garden and see what you think?"

Peter did as she suggested and turned to follow Laura. As he did so, she smiled at Toula and gave a knowing look to her daughter. After a complete tour of all the gardens, they sat on the rear patio and Laura brought drinks out for them.

Peter had asked a lot of relevant questions as they walked through the gardens. Laura was impressed with his knowledge of the climate and the plants that thrived within it. She could see how thrilled Peter was with the prospect of being in charge of these wonderful gardens, and thought he would be an excellent employee.

"Before I speak to you regarding salary, hours of work etc, I feel we have been a little less than honest with you," Laura remarked. Peter wondered what the let-down would be, as he really wanted this job. He then noticed how Toula looked at her mum and frowned.

"I need to come clean and tell you something," Laura continued. "Toula is our daughter, and although what she told you is true, yes, we have been looking for a gardener for some time, but I think Toula may have a soft spot for you."

"Will you cut it out, Mum? I am an adult and a qualified doctor. I am more than capable of making decisions about people I would like, or not like in my life," she demanded.

Peter looked a little shocked to discover that Toula was in fact a doctor, not that it really mattered, but then he looked pleased. He liked her. Not only was she indeed very beautiful, but he thought she was also a beautiful person on the inside.

Peter was offered the job, which he was very pleased to accept. He was even more pleased when Laura confirmed the salary he would be receiving. When Laura asked when he could start, he almost said "right now," as he was so enthusiastic about it.

"I am available whenever you want me to start," he told Laura, trying not to show too much excitement.

Laura thought for a moment. She could see how happy Toula was about Peter getting the job. It would be nice having him around.

"Come here on Monday morning, around nine," Laura instructed. "I can show you where everything is kept, regarding the garden. You two should go and have some fun together this weekend before the hard work begins."

Peter looked a little worried.

"Problem?" asked Laura.

"Not really," he replied. "I am just a little concerned as to whether I can find this place on Monday."

"I can bring you," Toula was quick to jump in, maybe a little too quick she thought later. "If we go swimming first, I can bring you from the beach, drop you off, and then I can go on to my surgery." Peter could not stop smiling. He looked delighted at the prospect of spending time with Toula.

"Right off you go, the two of you," Laura told them.

They got into Toula's car and drove out of the large gates, which opened automatically.

"I need to call at my house," Toula told Peter. "It's not far."

It certainly wasn't far. Her father, Nikos, had built a house for her only a matter of minutes from his and Laura's.

The house had the same automatic electric gates as her parents' house, with high walls built as an extra security measure. The garden was smaller than the house they'd just visited, but Toula had planned it herself to be a low maintenance garden, as she did not have a lot of time to tend it, given her job. She pulled up outside the front of the house and then opened the car door. She could see that Peter was impressed with her home.

"Do you want to come in whilst I sort out what I have to, and then we can go wherever you like," Toula asked, if a little awkwardly. Peter nodded, got out of the car and followed her to the front door. Toula opened it and let Peter in.

"Wow!" Peter announced, thinking the interior was fantastic. "You have a fabulous house," he remarked.

"My father built it for me. It's what Greek fathers do for their daughters," Toula told him.

"He must have had a lot of money to build this, along with his own house. He must be a millionaire," he laughed.

'If only you knew,' Toula thought to herself.

"Take a seat in the lounge. I won't be long," Toula instructed, pointing to a closed door.

Peter went in and was flabbergasted at the size of it. It was built on two levels, with full wall windows to take in the views over the garden and furnished with massive couches and oriental mats. The walls had large paintings hung on them, and shelves held large porcelain vases and ornaments.

A few minutes later, Toula returned, having changed from her swimwear and cover-up into a short sundress.

"Sorry, I was waiting for some important results to come through from the laboratory so that I could pass the information on to a patient," she said, impressing Pater. "All done and dusted now. Where would you like to go?"

"Perhaps we could go somewhere to eat, have a chat and get to know each other a little better," Peter suggested.

"Sounds good to me," Toula told him. They went back to the car. "Do you have a driving license?" she questioned.

Peter thought it was a strange question, seeing as he'd already told her he planned on buying a car, but "Sure," he replied, wondering why she'd asked. But then she passed him the keys to her car. "You want me to drive?" he said, surprised.

"Why not, the car's insured for anyone to drive and you did say you liked it. Give it a try," she said, climbing into the passenger seat beside him. Peter carefully put the car in gear and then drove it slowly down the drive. He couldn't keep the grin off his face as he did so.

"Where to, Madam?" he teased.

"My Place," Toula suggested. "We can eat there and then sit by the pool." Peter looked confused and seeing his look of confusion, Toula explained, "It's a restaurant called My Place," she laughed. "I wasn't inviting you back to my house for a meal!"

"My Place it is," Peter confirmed, now understanding.

Although he drove quite slowly through the village, Toula could see he would love to drive it faster.

"Perhaps next time, we can go a little further afield and you can drive us?" Toula said, not only making Peter smile, but giving herself butterflies at the prospect of spending more time with him.

They lunched at 'My Place' and then sat by the pool. They chatted for ages about all sorts of things, all the time laughing together and really enjoying each other's company.

"Perhaps I should be getting back now," Toula said, although really not wanting to leave Peter at all. He looked at her and smiled.

"How about we meet later and you tell me all about yourself and your family?" he suggested.

"And will you tell me about you and yours, should I agree?" Toula requested.

"It's a date," Peter smiled.

"Do you need me to drop you off on my way back? Although I don't know where you're staying," Toula observed.

"It's okay, I can walk from here. That's why I swim at Kastri," Peter told her.

"Well where shall we meet?" Toula asked. "If we're going to have a drink, I don't want to bring the car. I can easily get a lift down here."

"Let's go to Ficus. I have heard the food is excellent there," he suggested.

"Yes it is. I can tell you that from experience," she replied.

"Ficus it is then, around eight at the bar?" Peter smiled, already feeling excited about the rendezvous later.

"I'd better get a move on then," Toula told him.

Peter stood from his chair and kissed Toula on the cheek.

'That was a surprise,' she thought, although she very much enjoyed it.

"Bye then," was all she could say.

As she drove home, the kiss on her cheek felt like a bee sting. She couldn't stop touching it and heaved a deep sigh. Toula had to admit, she really liked Peter.

She showered and washed her hair, taking extra time to style her, sometimes unruly curls. She could not stop smiling, as she thought about, and looked forward to the upcoming evening with Peter.

The phone rang. It was her mum. "Is everything okay, Darling?" Laura asked. They regularly checked on her since the kidnap episode.

"Hunky Dory," Toula replied.

"Did you have fun this afternoon?" her mum asked.

"Of course, and before you ask if I am seeing Peter again, yes I am, but if you keep talking to me I'll be late meeting him."

"What's Peter's surname?" Laura asked. "I forgot to ask him this morning."

"I will find out for you," Toula promised. "Look, I am trying to get ready." She said this with a laugh, and Laura was so happy for her daughter.

"Have fun. Bye," Laura said, putting the phone down.

Toula finished her hair and makeup and took a quick glance in the mirror. The doorbell rang, and waiting outside was a punctual as ever, Babis, who was the designated driver to take her to Ficus.

They arrived at the restaurant and Toula could see Peter already seated and waiting at the bar.

"Thanks for the lift. See you soon," she said to Babis, as she eased herself out of the car. Surprisingly, Babis got out too.

"What are you doing?" Toula asked her brother.

"Just checking something out," he replied

'Ever the policeman, and always on duty,' she thought.

Toula expected him to go to see the Greek guys who worked there, but he headed straight for the bar. Peter was the only other person there, and Babis sat on the bar stool next to him.

"Good evening," Babis said politely to Peter.

Toula walked up to the other side of Peter, and was soon by his side. He turned to face her, and smiled when she'd reached him. He immediately stood up to greet her by kissing her on the cheek and pulling out the stool next to him. Toula glared at Babis, but annoyingly he just smiled back.

Peter was about to speak to Toula when Babis interrupted. "You're new around here, aren't you?"

"I've been here a couple of months," he told Babis, although confused by the question. "Why do you ask?"

Toula was on the edge of her stool, gesturing to Babis to stop what he was doing.

"Just interested," Babis replied, a little nonchalantly.

"Enough," Toula called out. Babis smiled as she continued telling Peter, "This is my cousin Babis. He's a policeman and he thinks he has to watch over me as if I'm still a little girl. Please, just ignore him."

Peter turned to Babis and offered his hand to shake and Babis shook it.

"Okay mate," he said to Peter. "It had to be done. I am sure Toula will tell you why." He stood preparing to leave. Before exiting the restaurant and heading back to his car, he turned and smiled at Toula, but she again glared at him.

"Have a good evening both of you," Babis said. "It's nice to have met you, Peter. I am sure we will see more of each other in the future, especially judging by Toula's face," he laughed and was gone.

Toula felt embarrassed about what had just happened. "Some cousins can be so annoying," she joked, but then, seeing the mystified look on Peter's face, she added. "I will tell you later, Peter," she promised.

"Shall we have a drink?" Peter said.

They moved later to the table which he'd booked earlier and after, they enjoyed a lovely meal. Toula insisted they went halves on the bill even though Peter protested that he'd been the one who'd invited her out this evening.

"Shall we take a walk," he invited, and Toula nodded.

They walked down to the seafront and along past Stamatia and Argo restaurants. As they passed Corner Café, the girls who worked there waved to Toula, wondering who she was with. They continued their walk over the little wooden bridge, and then went on the beach. Toula was so glad she had chosen to wear flat shoes.

Peter casually held her hand as they walked on past Royal Bay. It seemed quiet everywhere tonight. The moon began to rise in the sky, casting long reflections on the sea.

"Let's sit and watch the stars," Peter said as they approached a bench outside the water sports centre. They remained silent for a few moments, enjoying each other's company whilst gazing out to sea.

"Tell me all about you, Toula," Peter said eventually. "I want to know everything."

"There isn't that much to tell. I was born here on the island. As you know, my mum is English and my father is Greek. He owns a yacht building company which my brother Demetris now runs. I went to England to learn medicine, and upon my return, I worked at the paediatric centre in the village, which my father funded and my Uncle ran. I now have my own surgery, working as a general practitioner. I'm single and quite recently I was the victim of a kidnap." Upon hearing this, Peter was shocked.

"What!" he exclaimed. "You were kidnapped?"

"A young guy from the village kidnapped me and he asked my father for one million euros for my safe return."

"So, what happened? How could anyone pay that sort of ransom money?" Peter was anxious to discover.

"My ever-loving cousin saved the day by dressing as a priest. He confronted the guy who was wielding a knife at my father, and then at him. The kidnapper tried to escape with the money, but Babis had everything covered and my father got his money back."

"Wow. You must have been terrified?" Peter claimed.

"I didn't see it as I was bound and gagged and hidden in the church," Toula explained, but Peter couldn't take all this in.

"Now I see why your cousin is so protective of you. I see why he wanted to check me out. He must be a suspicious, but very special man," Peter suggested.

"Oh, he's special alright," she said laughing. "And to end my story," she carried on, "I belong to a very large Greek family, most of them living in very close proximity to me, who seem to know everything."

"Thanks for trusting me enough to tell me those things," Peter said.

"I will tell you one more thing," Toula said, "Because I rather expect someone else will tell you, if I don't." Peter wondered what was coming next, but didn't have to wait long before being astounded. "My father owns a company that builds super yachts. He is in fact a millionaire several times over."

"You mean your father is a multi-millionaire?" Peter asked.

"Yes he is," Toula admitted.

"But you are so normal," he said. He meant it as a compliment, and Toula accepted it as such.

Peter sat and held her hand. He then moved to put his arm around her. They sat in silence and Peter knew it had been difficult for her to tell him these things, and he felt such a huge amount of respect for her in doing so. He was beginning to really like this beautiful girl.

They looked up at the night sky. The stars were beginning to appear. "Look at the stars," Peter requested. "Stars always shine through the dark. They are brightest when the darkness is at its deepest."

Toula turned to look at him. "You are so lovely, Peter," she told him. She then moved close enough so she could kiss him like she'd wanted to for ages.

They walked back along the sand with their arms around each other. Although neither wanted the evening to end, Toula had promised to ring Babis to give her a lift home, and she didn't want to keep him up too late.

"There is still a full day of the weekend left before I start work. Can we spend it together?" Peter asked.

"I thought you'd never ask," Toula smiled. "Of course we should, as you haven't told me anything about yourself, and I want to know everything about you," she replied.

Babis arrived to take Toula home. He wound down the window and shouted to Peter. "I hope you were a complete gentleman," he challenged.

"Of course," Peter returned.

"Good," Babis stated. "I wouldn't want to arrest you!" Luckily, Peter could see he was joking.

"I am always a gentleman when I am with a beautiful lady," Peter smiled back at Babis. He then kissed Toula on the cheek and said, "Until tomorrow."

"Where shall we meet?" she hurriedly asked.

"Kastri beach," he shouted, as Babis drove away.

'What a night,' Peter thought, smiling happily to himself.

Babis dropped Toula off at her house, ensuring she went safely inside. He then drove off, knowing Poppy would be waiting for him to return.

Toula put the lights on as soon as she walked inside the house. Understandably, she still felt a little anxious after recent events, and now realised just now how alone she was. She wished Peter could be there with her.

As she undressed and climbed into bed, sleep evaded her. She couldn't stop thinking of the evening she'd just spent with Peter. Just thinking of his name brought a smile to her face.

She really did like this lovely young man, and yet she knew hardly anything about him.

She snuggled up under the covers and hoped he would tell her lots more about himself tomorrow.

"Goodnight Peter," she said out loud. "See you tomorrow," she smiled.

CHAPTER 16
A NEW HOME FOR PETER

Toula drove down to Kastri, but was surprised to see there was no sign of Peter. She felt really disappointed that he wasn't waiting for her. She sat on the sand and waited, but he still didn't come.

She was almost ready to get up and go when he appeared, walking down the beach at a fast pace. He went to her and kissed her on the cheek.

"I'm really very sorry for being late, Toula," he said, apologising profusely. He went to explain that the landlord where he was staying in the resort had told him that he must leave, as he was closing down all the apartments ready to refurbish them and get them ready for the next season.

Peter had to pack up all his belongings and had promised the landlord that he would return later that day to collect them, once he'd found somewhere else to stay. That is, until the time his parents arrived with a shipment of furniture for the empty house they'd bought.

Toula kissed him on the cheek and smiled. She was just relieved that nothing really bad had happened to him.

"I can ring a few people I know to see if they have any rooms available," she suggested.

"Thanks," Peter said, again apologetically. "Sorry to spoil the day for you."

"Nonsense," Toula remarked. "It's not a problem. You are here, and that's all that matters to me," she stressed, making peter feel like a very happy man.

They sat on the beach together, whilst Toula tried ringing some of her friends about a room for Peter. However, there seemed to be nothing available.

"Sounds like there's no room at the inn," Peter remarked, making a joke of a potentially serious problem.

"I'll ask the family and see what they can come up with," Toula suggested, seeing the slightly concerned look, now on Peter's face.

"Thank you," Peter said, speaking softly.

"Come on, you, let's go and get a coffee," Toula suggested. "We'll see if anyone gets back to us," she said.

They left the car in the car park and walked up the lane from the beach and went into My Place.

"Since we have nothing to do at the moment, why don't you tell me all about yourself," Toula invited, smiling.

"Okay but there isn't really much to tell you. I have one brother and one sister. I have lived in Ireland most of my life and I went to college. My parents bought a house here, and as a family we are moving here very soon. Also, thanks to you, I have found employment on the island, but my landlord has just thrown me out" he laughed as he offered the last snippet of information.

"I'm sure there is much more to you than that," Toula said, also laughing.

"Would you like to see the house my parents have bought?" Peter suggested. "We could go down to the beach at Limnionis to swim if you like?"

They walked back to Toula's car and she tossed the keys to Peter. He grinned and unlocked the door for her to get into the passenger seat. He drove up the road to the village and passed through it, taking a left turn at the junction which was signposted to Limnionis.

As he drove down the road towards the beach, he took a right turn and followed a narrow road for a few metres. In front of them was a newly built house. It was larger than Toula expected, and quite stylish in appearance.

"I have a key," Peter told her. "Do you want to come in and look inside?" he questioned. "There is no electricity or water connected yet, that's why I've been renting down in the resort."

"Of course," Toula replied.

As they wandered round the empty but freshly plastered rooms, Toula tried to imagine what it would look like when it was finished and furnished. It seemed there would be a large garden surrounding the house, and Peter had been given the project of designing and building it.

"We had a house in Ireland and still own property in France and Italy," he revealed. Toula was surprised when she heard this. "Mum likes Italy and dad likes France. It's as simple as that," he explained.

They took a little longer looking round, then locked the house up securely and returned to the car. They hadn't yet received any phone calls about available accommodation for Peter.

"Let's go and swim," Toula suggested.

Peter drove the car down the winding roads to the beach and harbour at Limnionis. As usual, there were fishermen cleaning their nets ready to take their little boats out and attempt to make a good catch to sell later.

There were a few couples on the sun loungers to the right hand, more sheltered cove so they walked to the left, where it was less protected and the waves were rolling in. There, they discarded their shorts and t-shirts and ran into the water, forgetting all their worries and just enjoying the fantastic waves which lifted them off their feet as they stood there. A game of splashing each other began, and their laughter could be heard all across the cove.

They waded ashore and dried themselves. As they did so, Toula's phone rang.

"This might be good news for you," she told Peter.

However, it wasn't good news at all. It seemed that every apartment was rented out. The problem being that many of them had been contracted with the big hotels, like Ikos, White Rock and Blue Lagoon, to rent out rooms for the workers at their establishments. They sat on the rocks at the entrance to the cove and mulled things over.

"It's only until my parents get here and get the services connected," Peter told her, beginning to lose heart.

"Let's not give up yet," Toula instructed, as her phone rang again. "See, I told you," she said as she answered it. Unfortunately, it was just her mother calling.

"Your phone had gone out of service so I was a bit concerned," Laura told her.

"I'm down at Limnionis," she told her mother. "The signal can often drop here. I'm with Peter and we have just been swimming, but I'm okay, don't worry about me."

"Sorry, I can't help it," Laura stressed. "I still worry about you, even though you're an adult. It's because I love you."

"I know. Now get off the phone. Stop worrying and let me enjoy my time with Peter," Toula pleaded, although grateful for her mother's obvious love and concern for her daughter.

"Love you," was Laura's parting comment.

"Love you too," Toula replied, ending the call.

"Sorry Peter, no joy with accommodation." Peter nodded.

They sat in silence for a few minutes, but then, suddenly, Toula had a moment of clarity.

"Okay Peter," she began, "this may seem a little crazy and a bit pushy, but I have several empty rooms in my house and I'm happy for you to use one until you get sorted."

Peter wasn't sure what to say, it would solve a problem in the short term. It was also close to where he would be working and Toula wouldn't have to ferry him to work and back each day. He could walk to Laura's home from Toula's house.

"Are you sure about this?" he did however ask.

Toula looked straight at him and said, "Look I'm not asking you to marry me or anything, I'm just trying to help. I would welcome having someone else in the house, because since the kidnapping, I haven't felt as comfortable there as I did before. It seems like a win-win situation to me. Now shall we go and collect your things?" she said, putting him on the spot.

Peter hesitated, but only for a second. "If you're really sure..." he began to say.

"If you don't stop asking me that, I will change my mind," she told him sternly.

"Thank you, Toula," Peter said, and he meant it.

They left Limnionis, but this time Toula drove. She took the back road that led back to the Pantheon Hotel before rejoining the main road. Peter then gave directions to the rented accommodation, where they collected what meagre belongings he had and put them into the boot of the car. They then drove back to Toula's house.

"I will have to give you pass codes and keys to get in and out of the house and garden," Toula told peter, and then added, "My dad is very keen on security."

Peter carried his things into the house and Toula led him to one of the bedrooms. Once she'd opened the door and Peter had put his things down, she showed him the door to the en-suite and gave him the security numbers for opening the patio doors which led to a small balcony. Peter was very impressed.

"It's like staying in a top hotel," he told her. "I really appreciate this, Toula."

"You are more than welcome," she happily told him.

"So, where do you sleep?" he questioned, but then immediately wished he hadn't.

"That's for me to know and for you to find out," she replied, feeling stupid as soon as she'd said it. It was a bit like treading on eggshells!

"Now," Toula continued, "I must let the family know about you before they get the wrong idea about your being here."

"And why would they do that?" Peter queried.

"Let's just say they are a bit overprotective of me at times," Toula stated.

"Yes, I saw that last night with Babis," Peter agreed.

"Sorry about that," Toula remarked.

"I truly thought he was going to arrest me." Peter admitted. They both laughed at the thought of this.

A little later in the day, Peter felt a bit sheepish as they headed for Toula's parents' house. When they arrived, Laura was pleased to see them and invited them in. Toula's father, Nikos, was home and he introduced himself to Peter.

"Hello Peter," Nikos began. "I believe you are starting work here tomorrow. My wife has told me how skilled and knowledgeable you are concerning gardening. Welcome aboard."

Peter began to relax a little, until the next question was asked. "And where are you staying on the island?"

Toula took the floor and butted into the conversation. "Peter is staying with me, Dad," she divulged.

Both her mum and dad looked at her as she continued. "It's okay and only temporary. He's only staying until either his parents arrive to open up the house they've bought, or until he finds alternative accommodation, because his landlord has asked him to leave."

"You've not been causing trouble, have you?" Nikos asked Peter jokingly. Peter was about to answer, but Nikos just held up his hand. "My daughter doesn't trust people easily, but she is usually a good judge of character. If she has invited you into her home, then she must trust you. And if she trusts you, then her mother and I both trust you. Do you need any help moving your things?"

"We have already moved into the house," Toula remarked.

"Blimey girl, you don't mess around," Nikos joked. This made Peter feel really happy to be in Toula's parents' company. They chatted for a while and then they left for home.

On the way back to his new accommodation, Peter couldn't help but notice that Nikos was an amputee and referenced it to Toula.

"I couldn't help but notice that your father has an artificial leg," he said.

"He was in a very bad accident and nearly lost his life. It happened just before he married my mother, but it has never stopped him living a full and active life. He is a real star," she proclaimed. "Once you get to know him you will realise what a good man he is, and a much-esteemed employer," she went on to say.

"I'm sure you will meet the rest of the family pretty soon, as they will all also want to check you out. I hope you know what you're letting yourself in for," thankfully for Peter, Toula laughed when saying this.

They spent the rest of the day together, but when it came to return to the house, it began to feel a little awkward. They both expressed the need for an early night, being that they were both starting work early the next day. They said their goodnights on the landing and Peter watched as Toula went into the room next to his.

Although he wished he was going in there with her, he was able to quickly shake the thought from his mind. However, unbeknown to Peter, at the same time, Toula went into her own room also wishing that he was coming in there with her. Only time would tell how their friendship would develop.

Every day they breakfasted together and passed each other on the landing. They left for work at the same time, came home and showered within minutes of each other. They then often went out to eat in the evening together. They were so much like a married couple, except for the fact that there was no intimacy between them, even though they both dreamed of the day when it would happen.

CHAPTER 17
YOU'RE A STAR

When Peter's parents finally arrived, along with the furniture and household items, they quickly arranged for electricity and water to be connected. Peter told them how he'd been staying at Toula's house in the village.

"It would be very nice to meet her, Son. She sounds like a lovely girl," they said.

"She is," Peter confirmed.

Peter's father went with him to collect the car that Peter had ordered. Although excited about this, he also felt sad that he no longer had to rely on Toula to drive him around. However, he thought he would miss being constantly with her and enjoying her company.

Peter took Toula to meet his parents, one sunny afternoon. All his family were sitting on the patio at the rear of the house when they arrived. She was feeling nervous about meeting them.

Peter's father stood up to welcome Toula and offered her his chair. She smiled and thanked him.

"It's lovely to meet you, Toula," Peter's mother said. "Peter has told us so much about you and the kindness your family has shown towards him. I would like to personally say thank you for that.

Let me introduce you to our family. This is, Richard, my husband," Richard smiled and nodded at Toula. "I am Frances," his mother announced, "and this is Stuart, Peter's younger brother. This here is Daisy, the baby of the bunch."

Introductions over, they began to chat about their move and the complications they'd met with trying to organise everything.

"Things seem to move so slowly," Frances told Toula.

"Tell me about it," Toula offered.

"It's not easy moving here," Frances stated.

"You are in Greece now. Everything here is avrio, manana, tomorrow," Toula advised with a smile. She was able to relax now and enjoy the friendly atmosphere.

"I'm sure we're going to enjoy living here, once we're all settled," Richard said.

At that moment, the phone rang. Although he tried to ignore it, eventually Richard answered it. Toula tried not to listen, but as the conversation continued, Richard got louder and louder, and more and more irate, until he slammed the phone down.

"Bloody incompetence," he hissed, and fell back into his chair. Before anyone could ask what the call had been about, Richard grabbed his chest and gasped at the pain that was searing through his body.

"What's wrong, Richard," Frances asked in blind panic, but he couldn't speak.

Toula knew what was happening and her role as a doctor took over any pleasantries.

"Peter, fetch my bag from the car. Stuart, call an ambulance and give them precise directions. Frances, do you have any aspirin?" Nobody moved.

"Do it now!" Toula demanded.

"Just who do you think you are speaking to?" Frances said incensed, thinking what a rude person Toula was.

"I am a doctor and your husband is having a heart attack," Toula confirmed. "We need to act immediately."

"Is my daddy dying? Please don't let him die," Daisy cried out hysterically.

Peter came back with Toula's bag. She searched through it looking for a hypodermic needle and a capsule of adrenaline. When she found what she was looking for, she rolled up Richard's sleeve and administered the drug.

Frances returned with an aspirin, which Toula took and put in Richard's mouth, encouraging him to chew it and swallow. She politely asked Stuart and Daisy to leave the room, as she was beginning to get quite concerned about Richard.

After taking his pulse, she spoke to him. He was quite incoherent when he tried to reply to her, but then suddenly he slumped in the chair.

Toula checked his breathing and heart rate. He'd stopped breathing and his heart rate was dropping.

"Peter, help me get him down on the floor," Toula shouted. Together, they lay Richard down and Toula commenced CPR.

"Chase up the ambulance," Toula shouted, as she continued to work on Richard, checking him and then continuing.

When the ambulance finally arrived, she handed him over to the paramedics, telling them what she'd given him and how long she'd been administering CPR.

Frances went in the ambulance with Richard, while Peter and Toula followed in her car. The ride to Kos hospital seemed like an eternity! When they finally arrived, Richard was rushed off to the resuscitation room, whilst Frances stood outside in the corridor and wept.

Eventually one of the emergency doctors came out to the three of them, knowing they'd been waiting but with them not knowing what was happening. The emergency doctor recognised Toula and came to speak with her.

"Hi Toula, is this a member of your family? "the doctor questioned.

"No, but this is his wife," Toula advised. "Would you like to speak to her alone?" she asked, hoping it wasn't bad news.

The doctor turned to Frances and broke the news. "Your husband is stable now and breathing normally. We will need to do more tests to find out what has caused the attack and it may mean a trip to Athens for some corrective surgery, but we will know more a little later."

Frances nodded but was unable to speak, as the emergency doctor looked at Toula and smiled.

"Given the timeframe, had you not been there it could have been a completely different story," he told Toula. "Well done, Doctor," he said, putting his hand on Toula's shoulder. Then turning to Frances, he announced. "You have a lot to thank this young lady for." With this said, he turned and returned to the emergency room.

Frances came to Toula and hugged her. "Thank you Toula. I am sorry I was rude to you. You really are a real star. Thank you."

Richard was taken to Athens for a stent to be inserted into his heart. The prognosis was good, and life returned to normal for him and the rest of Peter's family.

The family were soon able to move into their new house in Kefalos, and Peter's room was now ready for him to move into. After staying with Toula at her home, it now saddened him to think he would have to leave her house. He started to gather up his things, but Toula heard him and went up to see what he was doing.

"You're going then?" she questioned.

"I guess I have to" Peter replied, with deep sadness in his voice.

"Do you have to?" Toula asked. "Do you really? Are you sure?" Peter looked straight at her as she carried on saying, "We know we can live together in the same house and get along just fine, don't we? So what's wrong with us living together now? That is unless you would prefer to go and live with your family."

Peter very much wanted to stay with Toula in this house. "You mean as a couple, a proper couple?" he queried a little confused.

"Well yes. We would have to try it out, so we could, couldn't we," Toula suggested.

"Yes, but when?" Peter asked hopefully.

"Whenever you like," she replied.

"How about now," Peter said, winking at her. "How about right now," he said, beaming all over his face.

"I'm game, so your place or mine?" Toula remarked, gesturing at the pile of belongings on Peter's bed and smiling at him. "Looks like it'll have to be mine," she smiled.

Hand in hand, they left the chaos in Peter's room and moved into Toula's room. Peter had never been in here before. Everything was neat and tidy. Her bed was neatly made with cushions scattered all over it. Peter made the first move and held Toula's hand.

"Are you sure?" he asked, trembling a little with excitement.

"I could change my mind if you keep asking me that," she said, as she took him hand in hand towards the bed.

Moments later, they took the step from friendship to intimacy. Both had wanted it, both had dreamed of it, and now they gave themselves willingly to each other.

Peter later told his parents that he'd changed his mind and wasn't coming to live with them. In their minds, they already knew this would be the case, and were happy for him to be with Toula. They could see what the pair meant to each other.

Toula went to see her parents feeling a little like a naughty child who had done something wrong and betrayed her parents' trust, but when she tried to tell them they just smiled.

"What took you so long?" Laura said. "Peter is a lovely boy who will always take good care of you. And it goes without saying that we know you two will be immensely happy together."

"Thanks Mum. Thanks Dad," Toula gushed, knowing she had the best parents in the world.

Nikos looked at his daughter. At this minute he knew that he was now no longer the most important man in her life, and he felt a little sad. However, he liked Peter and knew his daughter had found the true happiness she'd always wished for.

"Is there to be another Greek wedding?" Laura asked.

"Not yet" Toula told Laura. "Not yet, Mum, but maybe one day soon."

CHAPTER 18
MORE FLOWERS FOR
JENNY'S GARDEN

Five months after both Poppy and Kali had announced that they were expecting, they travelled to Athens together with their partners. Everything was ready and waiting for their arrival at the hospital, and fortunately they were put in adjacent rooms.

Both fathers looked quite nervous, so were reassured by one of the nurses that everything was going according to plan. Babis and Jacques sat for a time with their wives, and then went into the corridor.

"How is she doing?" Babis asked about his sister.

"She's fine, how about Poppy?" Jacques replied.

"She seems okay. They say it won't be long," said a really nervous Babis.

"That's good. Better get back in there now." Jacques stated.

"Me too," and when this nervous conversation ended, both expectant fathers' returned to their rooms.

Time dragged as they watched their partners dealing with the fierce contractions that were coming quicker and quicker. It had been several hours and the two expectant mums were getting tired.

Their partners felt like two spare parts, each one only able to hold the hand of his wife, offer a few drops of water, or place a wet flannel on their foreheads.

With each contraction, the women dug their nails into their respective partner's hand. Both men tried not to flinch, as it was clear that this pain was insignificant compared to what their wife was going through.

First to be born was Poppy and Babis' baby, a boy, healthy and strong, and with a very loud cry. Jacques heard the cry and went out quickly to congratulate Babis.

There had been little progress for Kali and there was talk of a possible Caesarean Section. The doctors, having consulted with each other decided not to follow that course, as at the moment neither of the twins was in distress.

The very same evening as Poppy's baby had been delivered, but much later the first of the twins was born. Like Poppy's baby it was also a boy, looking a little small but healthy just the same.

A while later, the second twin made an appearance. This time, it was a girl, and bigger than her brother. Both of the twins had lovely jet black hair.

Kali and Poppy had done tremendously well, encouraged as they were, by their nervous husbands.

A couple of days later, the four returned to their beloved island of Kos, where the family waited to meet the next generation.

Babis and Poppy had chosen the name, Aithan Gareth, meaning 'strength and determination' for their son.

Kali and Jacques decided that in honour of the founders of the family dynasty, they would call their daughter, Jenny Valentina, named after her great-great grandmother, Jenny, and Jacques mother. They named their son, Jean Pierre, named after Jenny's first husband, John, and also Jacques father.

And so, a family dynasty that was begun by Jenny, a brave lady, who came to Kefalos in order to keep a promise made to her first husband, John, had been blessed with another new generation.

They'd always been a family who stood together through tragedy and trauma, helped each other and gave support to each other through good times and bad, but more than anything else, they were a family who shared love.

"I wonder if Jenny is looking down now on this family which she created all those years ago," Laura asked.

"I'm sure she is, and she will have the biggest smile," Nikos advised.

"To Jenny," everyone raised a glass high into the air and toasted.

Laura walked away from the rest of the family to get some alone time. She looked up to the sky and softly mouthed, "Thank you, Mum. Look at this wonderful family you and Dad created. Thank you so much." As she returned to the family, Laura felt truly blessed.

Life and love continued to thrive within this family in Kefalos, but that's another story - maybe.

THE END

Printed in Great Britain
by Amazon